STRUGGLE WITH SILENCE

To Julie, whose beauty shines inside and out.

"He has made everything beautiful in its time; also, He has put eternity into man's mind, yet so that he cannot find out what God has done from the beginning to the end" (Ecclesiastes 3:11).

Thank you for being a friend.

THE CAPITAL CREW

STRUGGLE WITH SILENCE

JEFFREY
ARCHER
NESBIT

VICTOR BOOKS®
A DIVISION OF SCRIPTURE PRESS PUBLICATIONS INC.
USA CANADA ENGLAND

THE CAPITAL CREW SERIES
Crosscourt Winner
The Lost Canoe
The Reluctant Runaway
Struggle with Silence

Cover illustration by Kathy Kulin-Sandel

Library of Congress Cataloging-in-Publication Data:

Nesbit, Jeffrey Asher.
    Struggle with silence / Jeffrey Asher Nesbit.
        p.   cm. — (The Capital crew series)
    Summary: Cally James tries to protect his siter Jana when she
becomes involved with a gang leader seeking revenge on Cally.
    ISBN 0-89693-132-3
    [1. Brothers and sisters — Fiction. 2. Tennis — Fiction. 3. Chris-
tian life — Fiction.]   I. Title. II. Series
    PZ7.N4378St   1991
    [Fic] — dc20   91-4708
                                                                          CIP
                                                                          AC

1 2 3 4 5 6 7 8 9 10 Printing/Year 95 94 93 92 91

VICTOR BOOKS
A division of SP Publications, Inc.
Wheaton, Illinois 60187

Mom should never have let Jana talk her into it. But Mom's got a soft heart, especially when it comes to Jana.

Which means, of course, that Jana is on the phone now all the time. And I mean *all* the time. She's always whispering into it, like she's part of a conspiracy or something.

She's never more than a few feet away from the phone. I think she's afraid that it might ring more than once and that the person who's calling will hang up before it rings the second time.

Sure. Everybody's always dying to talk to Jana. They'd let it ring a hundred times.

"But *why?*" I asked Mom one night, when Jana had been locked away behind her bedroom door, jabbering away for hours. "Why does Jana get to have her own telephone, in her room, when no one else does?"

"Look at it this way, Cally," Mom said reasonably. "Is there any way you're going to keep your sister off the phone?"

"Nope. Not in a million years."

"So, if that's the case, would you rather have Jana talking on the phone out in the middle of the living room while you're trying to watch 'Monday Night Football,' or in her and Karen's room where you can't hear her?"

"But . . ."

"Play fair," Mom insisted. "Answer my question, first."

"Well, 'course I'd rather have her somewhere else. It drives me nuts to hear her talkin' about all that junk all the time."

"So you think it's a good idea that she now has her own phone, where she isn't bothering the rest of the family?"

"Oh, I guess," I grumbled. "But it's still not fair, really. No one else gets their own phone."

"No one else uses it as much as she does, Cally."

"I know," I growled. "But it still gets to me that she's allowed to have her own phone, no matter what you say."

"It's the only way. We can't keep her off the phone."

Mom's right, of course. There's no way you're going to keep my sister off the telephone. No way at all.

I know Jana's really pretty and all of that. But what's crazy is that most of the calls aren't from boys, they're from her girlfriends. That's what drives me absolutely bonkers.

I'd understand it if she had all these boys calling her all the time. That would make sense. I could almost live with that. Mom would go crazy then, but I don't think I would.

No, what drives me up the wall is that all of Jana's girlfriends call and talk about this boy, or that boy, and isn't he cute, and does he like someone, and on and on and on. Then they always seem to ask Jana to go talk to some boy for them.

Jana and Karen started going to Roosevelt Junior High with me this fall. Jana had already made about a billion friends after the first week of school. They all hung out around her locker.

Karen kept to herself, mostly. She was still having a tough time getting over the incident during the summer with Dad. She still couldn't believe Dad had sort of gone over the edge. I figured it would just take some time, that she'd eventually get past it.

Karen was pretty tough. She'd bounce back. But, until she did, Jana would have no one looking out for her, like Karen always had. Which left *me* to keep an eye on her, to make sure she didn't get into too much trouble.

So, what I did was change the way I walked to my classes. I figured out a way to wander past Jana's locker between every class. I think Jana knew what I was doing, but she didn't say anything. She always seemed to be surprised to see me when I showed up or walked past.

It isn't a big deal. It's not like I'm her guardian or anything. I'm just her slightly older brother, that's all. If I don't look out for her, who will? Somebody has to look out for her, because Jana won't look out for herself. She'd walk right into a tornado without thinking, I'll bet.

Which is just about what happened when she ran into Tommy Kimble. I knew he was *big* trouble the first time I met him. What I didn't know was that he'd be *our* trouble.

I first met "Tommy Gun" Kimble in the restroom closest to the boys' locker room. I almost never go in that restroom, not if I can help it. It's where all the kids who smoke hang out. It always smells horrible in there.

But I had no choice, really. It was the nearest safe haven. Elaine Cimons, my Bible study partner, was walking down the hallway from the other end, her arms full of pamphlets. I was sure that if she saw me she'd ask me to help her hand the stuff out.

It's not that I'm against all the stuff that Elaine always hands out during school. Actually, a lot of what's in those little books she always carries around is great. They explain the Bible and who Jesus is and what happens when we die in a way anyone can understand.

No, what I can't stand is standing around in the hallway at school passing those little books out to other kids. Elaine doesn't seem to mind at all. She sort of glows when she does it.

I go a little crazy inside just thinking about it. I don't think I'll be able to ever really talk about why I became a Christian. And I *know* I'm not ready to stand around and tell other kids why they should too.

Which is why I ducked into the restroom near the boys' locker room in a big hurry. I just sort of lunged through the door and stood there for a second.

I almost gagged. The air was thick with smoke. I could hardly see through the haze.

There must have been a dozen boys crammed into the place, sucking away on cigarettes like they were about to walk to the gallows. Most of their clothes were in tatters—deliberately, of course. Most of them had long hair. A couple of them had hardly any.

"Hey, dude, got a bum?" this one kid asked me.

I glanced at him, one eye cocked. "What?"

"A bum, man, d'ya got a bum?"

I looked at him like he was crazy. I had no idea what he was talking about. He wasn't smoking a cigarette, and he had his hand stretched out toward me. "I don't think so," I said finally.

This kid gave me a curious look. "Dude, you from outer space or *what?* Whatcha in here for if you ain't got nothin' I can bum?"

That's when I figured it out. He wanted to "bum," or borrow, a cigarette from me. Sometimes I'm a little slow on the draw.

"Sorry," I said quickly. "I don't smoke."

This kid, whose greasy long hair covered up one of his eyes and who looked like he hadn't taken a bath in at least a week, flipped one of his locks over his shoulder the way a girl does. "For real?" he asked.

Another kid spoke up before I could answer. He was leaning up against the only stall in the small room. "Squirrel, you dingus, don't you know who that is?" this second kid asked.

"Squirrel" looked back at the second kid—who had his own long hair pulled back in a ponytail and who was dressed all in leather—like he was crazy too. "How'm I supposed to know every kid who walks in here?"

"You ain't supposed to know *every* kid," he answered. "But this is Cally James."

Squirrel jerked his head around and stared at me. I felt like a bug under a microscope. "C'mon, for real, dude?" he asked me. "Cally James, the tennis guy?"

"Yeah, I play tennis," I answered uneasily. I was beginning to feel like I'd wandered through a door into another dimension.

"You play tennis, all right!" said a third kid, in between one of his drags. "Big time. I've seen ya play."

"Man, he doesn't just play tennis," said the kid with the ponytail. "He won the national championship."

I stared hard at the kid with the ponytail. There had been just a hint of something in his voice, like it wasn't any kind of a big deal to win a national tennis championship. Well, maybe it wasn't to him.

"Dude, you won, like, the national championship?" Squirrel asked, clearly impressed.

I just nodded. I wasn't here to win over any fans. I just wanted to hang out here a few seconds more, long enough to let Elaine Cimons get around the corner.

" 'Course, Evan Grant is probably better," said the kid with the ponytail, his lip bunched in a faint curl, which was hard to see through the cigarette that sort of dangled from his lips.

"Maybe so," I shrugged.

"And I'll bet I could take ya too, if I practiced a little," said the kid with the ponytail.

"Fer sure, Tommy Gun, fer sure," one kid said, bobbing his head up and down like a puppet.

Nearly all the other kids in the room started nodding emphatically, agreeing with him. It was incredible. I almost started laughing. These kids had lost it.

"I don't think so," I said quietly.

"Nah, I'm sure I could," Tommy Gun sneered. "Little practice, I'm there."

I didn't answer right away. There wasn't any point to it, really. Tommy Gun, who was clearly the "leader" in here, was so far gone it wasn't even funny.

"Yeah, tennis ain't so hard," another kid said. "Tommy Gun could take him, with a little practice."

All the kids started bobbing their heads again, right on cue. I sighed to myself. This was crazy. I had to do something.

"Tommy Gun, you could practice from now until the end of the school year, and you'd *still* never even take a single point off me," I said, staring directly at him. I couldn't throw the gauntlet down any harder than that.

The whole room went still. The heads stopped bobbing. I could feel the walls closing in.

Tommy Gun leaned away from the stall. He took his half-burned cigarette from his mouth, holding it expertly between his thumb and forefinger. He flicked it away from him, hard. It slammed into the wall and sent a cascade of orange sparks in all directions.

The butt dropped to the floor, still smoldering. Glancing around furtively, Squirrel reached down quickly and scooped it up.

Tommy Gun moved through the haze slowly. A couple of the kids stepped out of the way. He stopped when he was right in front of me. He stared at me. I stared back, eyeball for eyeball. No way was I giving any ground to a punk like this. No way.

"This is my place, man," Tommy Gun said through clenched jaws. "Nobody talks to me like that in here."

"I just did," I said evenly.

"You think I'm foolin'?"

"No, but I know for sure you couldn't take a point off

of me in a tennis match," I said. "No matter how much you practiced."

I could almost see the hair stand up on the back of his neck. All eyes were on him now. If he backed down now, well . . .

"One week from Saturday," he said finally.

"High noon?" I joked. "On Roosevelt's courts?"

"Sure, why not?" shrugged Tommy Gun.

"That like twelve o'clock?" Squirrel asked.

"Yeah, you moron!" Tommy Gun snapped.

"What are we playin' for?" I asked.

Tommy Gun paused for a second. "I take a point off you in a set, you gotta supply me for a week," he said.

"Supply you?" I asked.

"Cigs, man!" Tommy Gun snorted, tapping his shirt pocket, where he kept his pack.

I nodded. "Okay, you're on. But what if I win?"

"You won't," Tommy Gun said.

I almost smiled. "But let's just pretend. What if I win every point in the set?"

"I'll stay outta your way for a week," he said, grinning viciously.

"Seems fair," I said. "See ya a week from Saturday. Don't be late." I turned and headed for the door.

"You're goin' down!" Squirrel called out after me.

"I don't think so," I said over my shoulder and walked out the door, the cool, fresh air of the hallway hitting me full in the face. The door to that strange land slammed shut behind me.

Now, it's almost impossible to win every, single point in a tennis match. That's the reality. No matter how bad someone is, you're still bound to plunk at least one shot into the net during the set.

Unless you change the way you play. Unless you play it safe, making doubly sure you hit everything back into your opponent's court and that you never take any chances.

I talked it over with Chris, and he agreed with me. If I played it safe, I could actually pull it off. It would allow Tommy Gun to stay in the match a little—to actually return a few of my shots—but that was okay. As long as I won every point, I didn't mind letting him stay with me on a few of the points.

"It's a pretty dumb bet, though, Cally," Chris told me after dinner that night, while we were outside tossing a football around.

"Why?"

" 'Cause I don't see how you can actually do it," he said. "And when you lose to the scuzzbucket, he'll lord it over you forever."

"But I *won't* lose the bet," I said, grim-faced.

Chris tossed the football high and to my left, forcing me to bolt over to get it. "Then you'd better practice," he said.

"I practice all the time."

"No, I mean practice a set the way you'll have to play against this . . . this—what's his name?"

"Tommy Gun."

"Yeah, Tommy Gun. . . . What kind of a name is that?"

"I dunno. They all seem to have nicknames like that."

"Yeah, well, anyway, you should practice playing safe."

"Why? I can take that clown."

"Man, Cally!" Chris said, zinging the ball back at me. "I know you can. But you've probably never tried to play a match where you pull back on your shots a little. You almost always hit out as hard as you can."

Chris was right, of course. I did always hit out. That was the way I did everything. I played as hard as I could. It was the only way to push the shadows back, to conquer the fear that always tried to enshroud you.

"So I have to practice?"

"Yeah, and I'll help you," grinned Chris.

"You will?"

"Sure. I'll just play with my left hand and hit really horrible shots. You'll have to play it safe on every shot you return."

I lofted the football high and deep; Chris turned and loped after it easily, gracefully. He caught it over one shoulder easily. He was beginning to develop into quite an athlete, I thought. Someday he would start to challenge me. Maybe soon.

"All right. Thanks," I called out. "So when do we start?"

"Right now," Chris said. He pulled the ball toward his chest and started to gallop right at me. I squared my shoulders and got set to tackle him.

Chris cut left, then right, just as he got to me. I went

for the first cut, and Chris went right past me. I never laid a hand on him.

"You're gettin' slow in your old age," Chris said as he continued to run toward the house.

I didn't say anything. I just turned and sprinted after him. Chris didn't stand a chance. I'd catch him by the time he got to the stairs leading up to the loft. Then he'd pay for that last, little move.

* * * * *

We practiced until it got dark. Boy, was Chris right. It was hard to change my game, to just play it safe. It went against everything I'd taught myself.

Even playing with his left hand, Chris was able to take a few points off of me. I double-faulted once. I tried to angle a backhand too much on one point and hit it wide. I pushed a volley into the net on another. And I hit one of Chris' feeble, left-handed serves deep on one point.

"That's ridiculous," I said in disgust after the practice set. "Those were all dumb mistakes."

"Yep, they were."

"So how can I actually do this?"

"Ah, you'll get the hang of it. No problem."

"You think so?"

"If you set your mind to it, you'll do it," Chris said.

"There's no way I'm gonna let this guy beat me," I answered, slamming the racket into my bag for emphasis.

"Then don't let him."

"I think I'll hit all second serves, so I won't double fault."

"Prob'ly smart."

"And I'll hit topspin to keep the ball in the middle of the court all the time. That way I can't hit it long."

"Makes sense."

"And I won't try to angle my shots."

Chris nodded. "Then you won't hit it wide."

I looked at my younger brother. We were both grinning from ear to ear. We were both thinking exactly the same thing.

"I can actually do this," I said.

"No, you *will* do it," he corrected me.

"Exactly. It'll be great."

"No, it'll be crummy while you're playing. It'll be great after you've finished and the guy hasn't taken a point off of you."

Chris came with me to the match. He was the only one I'd told about the match, so I figured he'd be the only one cheering me, against Squirrel and the others I'd seen through the haze in the boys restroom.

We showed up about a half an hour early. I wanted to get in a little practice before the match started. I had to be sharp right from the first point. I couldn't give anything away.

They started to show up right after we did. The fans, I mean. And not Tommy Gun's fans. *My* fans.

"Crush him, Cally!" a kid I'd never seen before called out to me through the chain-link fence.

"Yeah, wipe him out," said a girl sitting nearby.

When the stands were about half-full, I motioned to Chris to join me at the net. "What's the deal here?" I asked him, totally dumbfounded at the turnout.

Chris glanced over his shoulder at the fans. "It looks like the word got around."

"But it's just a stupid, little match."

"No, it isn't," Chris said. "I'll bet you this guy Tommy Gun's been poundin' on kids for a while. Now you come along and you're about to clean his clock. They just wanna be there when it happens."

I looked over at the gathering crowd. Chris could be right. In the past week, I'd noticed some funny looks in the hallway. Nobody had said a word, and I hadn't really thought about it. But it made sense, looking back.

And I'd asked around a little about Tommy Gun, now that I knew who he was. Chris was right on target. Tommy Gun was a bully, big-time. Now that he was an eighth-grader, he especially liked to terrorize the seventh-graders.

"This is kind of lunatic," I said to Chris.

"Not kind of," Chris answered.

"I guess I'd better win."

"I guess you'd better."

There was a sudden murmur in the small crowd of kids. A moment later, Chris and I both heard it. It sounded like the rumble of a big airplane. *Thump, thump, thump* it went.

The first bike turned the corner, followed by another and another and another. They were all making that same sound—*thump, thump, thump*—as they rolled toward the tennis courts.

Tommy Gun came first. He was flanked by Squirrel. The others I'd seen in the restroom followed in their wake.

As the bikes got closer, I could see what was making the sound. They'd all taken cards and stuck them through the spokes of their bikes. The cards were held in place with clothespins.

They all pulled into the parking lot at the same time. Their bikes were actually making a lot of noise. They almost sounded like motorcycles, even if they didn't look like Harley-Davidsons.

Most of them were dressed in black. A few had skulls painted on their jackets. A couple of them wore Viking helmets.

"Oooh, they're *bad*," I said, laughing.

"Looks sort of silly, if you ask me," Chris said.

Tommy Gun was dressed all in black, from head to toe. He was wearing jackboots, leather pants, and a flak jacket. Not exactly your everyday tennis outfit. I was wearing shorts and a cotton shirt.

"How's he gonna play tennis in that stuff?" I asked Chris, nodding toward Tommy Gun, who was walking somewhat stiffly toward the courts.

"Beats me."

When they were courtside, Tommy Gun's "fans" came right through the gate with him. They all started to take seats around the court where Chris and I were practicing. They ringed the entire court, and then sat down Indian-fashion. It was a little daunting.

Tommy Gun still hadn't looked at me or said anything. He turned to Squirrel instead and held out his hand; Squirrel promptly handed him the racket he'd been carrying. Tommy Gun took it, stared at it for a second, and then walked to the court opposite me.

"Do you wanna warm up?" I called out.

"Nope. Let's rock and roll," he answered back.

I looked back at Chris. He just shrugged, and started to walk off the court. He grabbed a seat on the ground in between two of Tommy Gun's fans.

It was just about then that the kids who'd come out on my behalf began to file through the gate as well. If Tommy Gun's fans could come in and try to intimidate me, well, then, I guess they figured they could come in and try to make Tommy Gun nervous.

"You don't have a prayer," I heard one kid say to Tommy Gun as he passed by. Tommy Gun didn't answer.

My fans spaced themselves out, clustering in between his gang. While they were getting themselves situated, I called out to Tommy Gun again. "You want the first serve?"

He waved his racket at me. "Nah, it's all yours. Knock yourself out, dude."

I nodded, and pocketed one of the two balls I held in my hand. I rolled the third ball against the net and walked toward the back line on my side.

"First serve?" I yelled. Tommy Gun nodded as he took his place opposite me. He was standing erect, the racket held limply off to one side.

I thought about blistering my first serve to start the match. He'd never even see it, much less touch it. Then I spotted Chris out of the corner of my eye. He was shaking his head back and forth. I grinned. He knew exactly what I was thinking. Play it safe. Don't be foolish.

I hit my second serve to Tommy Gun to start the match, a heavy topspin serve that kicked easily into the center of the service court and bounded high toward Tommy Gun's forehand.

Tommy Gun raised his racket and took a vicious swipe at it. He caught it with the top of his racket and the ball jumped off it. The ball screamed past me and slammed into the fence behind me before coming back down to earth.

"Yeah!" Squirrel yelled at the top of his lungs. "Way to cream it!"

I glanced over at Tommy Gun as I retrieved the ball. He was grinning from ear to ear, obviously pleased with himself. Well, he had gotten his racket on the ball. And I guess he figured that he'd get lucky on one of those returns and actually get it back in the court on my side.

If he did, it certainly would be tough to return it. Tommy Gun was obviously trying to hit it as hard as he could. And why not? All he had to do was get one point, just hit one ball in and hope I couldn't return it.

On the fourth and final point of the first game, one of Tommy Gun's screamers finally landed on my side of the court, deep and to my backhand. It looked like a sure winner.

Except that I'd already moved over in that direction, anticipating the flight of the ball. I took the ball on the rise and returned it easily with my backhand, a nice topspin back to his own backhand.

Tommy Gun scrambled toward the ball, a look of shock crossing his face. I guess he'd figured that all he had to do was get one ball back and the match would be over. He probably never considered that he might have to play the rest of the point.

He flailed helplessly with his own feeble backhand. The ball ticked the edge of his racket and hopped away. He'd lost the final point and the first game.

My fans erupted with ragged cheers. "Go for it, Cally!" yelled one. "Take him down!"

I acknowledged their cheers with a slight nod of my head. I began to walk toward the net to change sides.

"Whatcha doin'?" Tommy Gun yelled at me.

"Changin' sides," I answered back.

"Why?" he asked suspiciously.

"You always change sides after odd-numbered games," I said.

"That's stupid," Tommy Gun said. "I like this side."

"Yeah, stay on your own side, dude," yelled one of Tommy Gun's pals.

"Fine by me," I shrugged. "If you want that side, it's all yours."

I tossed Tommy Gun the ball in my pocket, flipped the one against the net over to him, and then walked back to the service court on my side.

Tommy Gun tossed a ball high in the air and swung as hard as he could. It landed a moment later in the court beside ours. He took a second ball and again swung as hard as he could, with just about the same result.

"Double-fault," I yelled.

"He knows that!" Squirrel yelled at me.

"Rip it, dude!" yelled one of Tommy Gun's fans.

Tommy Gun ripped it. This one was a little closer. It was only out by twenty feet. "Got any more balls?" he called out.

"Nope," I said. "You only play with three, and they're over in the next court."

"Well, go get 'em, then," he barked.

I loped over to the next court, flicked them off the ground between the side of my foot and the racket, and then plunked them over to Tommy Gun. He scrambled to gather the three balls up as they rolled toward him.

The next game, Tommy Gun almost got one of his serves in. On the third point in the game, his serve landed just five feet behind the service court. I caught the ball and then hit it back to him, easily.

"My point!" Tommy Gun yelled. "I win!"

I looked at him like he'd lost his mind. "What are you talkin' about? The ball was out by five feet."

"No, it wasn't," Tommy Gun said as he started to walk to the side of the court. "It was way inside the line."

That's when I realized what Tommy Gun must have thought. He must have figured he only had to get his serve in on my side of the court. He probably didn't know that you had to get each serve into a specific quarter of the court.

"Tommy Gun, serves have to land in these two box-es," I told him, gesturing to the two service courts in front of me on my side. "You serve to opposite boxes."

Tommy Gun glared at me. He glanced down at the lines on his side of the court, mulling it over.

"I knew that!" he finally snapped. "You sure my serve was out?"

"Yes, it was out," I answered, and returned to the baseline.

Tommy Gun walked back to his side and stared hard at the service courts across the net from him. I could see what he was thinking. He was wondering how in blue blazes he was going to get his serve into one of those boxes. It was a daunting task.

On his final serve, he drilled the ball into the ground, a good five feet short of the net. In disgust, Tommy Gun flung his racket up against the fence, nearly taking a kid's head off.

"Another racket," he yelled at Squirrel.

"That's the only one we brought," Squirrel answered sheepishly.

"Then get it," Tommy Gun said sullenly.

Squirrel scrambled to his feet, hustled over to the fence, and retrieved the racket. He ran it over to Tommy Gun, who accepted it with a scowl.

"You can do it, Tommy Gun!" Squirrel encouraged him.

"Oh, shut up," he answered.

I promptly put my next four serves in with ease. Tommy Gun never even came close to returning one of them. He was so mad he couldn't even see straight. Balls were careening in every direction.

My fans were cheering wildly now with every point. It was obvious, even to Tommy Gun's fans, that it would take something of a miracle for him to win a point.

He almost got one in the fourth game on his serve. On the third point, one of his serves ticked the top of the net and dribbled over onto my side. Tommy Gun let out a yell of joy and tossed his racket high into the air.

"I won! I won!" he yelled as the racket came crashing to the ground.

"Let serve," I said back to him, waiting for the yells from his fans to subside.

"What? What did you say?" Tommy Gun asked, calming down almost instantly. His fans were still yelling.

"On your serve, if the ball hits the net and lands in the court safely, you serve it over," I said. "It's called a 'let' serve."

"Hey, you can't make up the rules as you go along," Squirrel complained, catching on that maybe his leader hadn't actually won. "Tommy Gun won that point, fair and square."

"No, he didn't," Chris said back to Squirrel. "You're the goofball who doesn't know the rules."

Squirrel bristled and started to move toward my brother. I dropped my racket instantly and walked toward Squirrel. "Don't even think about it," I said to Squirrel.

"I can take care of myself," Chris said.

Squirrel looked at Chris, at me, then back at Chris. He shrugged, and stopped in his tracks. "No problem, dude. It's cool," he said.

"It'd better be," I said, my eyes blazing.

I picked up a ball and tossed it to Tommy Gun. "Your serve again," I said. "Let's go."

Tommy Gun caught the ball and watched me retrieve my racket. Then he turned and went back to his side of the court.

There was really only one more tense point. In the sixth and final game of the set, on his serve again,

Tommy Gun finally got a serve in. The ball came screaming over the net, landed in the service court, and skidded away hard to my forehand side.

I was just barely able to get my racket on it, just enough to send a looping forehand back, deep, to his own forehand. Tommy Gun was better prepared for the return this time, but he still hit it out by a mile.

Two points later, I'd won the set. On the last point, Tommy Gun tried to hit his serve so hard the ball actually sailed over the fence and into the parking lot. It was a fitting end to one of the most bizarre tennis matches I'd ever played. I'd won 6-0, and I hadn't given up a point.

Tommy Gun did not acknowledge defeat. He simply stalked off the court, motioning to his now-silent followers to exit the court with him.

"Next time!" Tommy Gun yelled at me as he aimed his boot at the kickstand on his bike. Squirrel just shook his fist at me.

"I knew you could do it," Chris said to me as we both watched the cycle gang roar off into the sunset, their cards flapping against their spokes madly.

"I'm glad you did," I answered. "I wasn't so sure. That guy's crazy. I never knew what he was going to do next."

5

You know, it's funny. I won a national champion-ship in tennis, and almost no one at school knew about it. Not really. Some of the kids knew I'd done something pretty interesting in tennis, but not much more than that.

Now, because I'd blanked some kid with a ponytail, I was famous. It seemed like everybody at school had heard about it. I kept half-expecting them to announce the score over the loudspeaker.

"In a dramatic and often tense match Saturday on Roosevelt's tennis court complex, Cally James defeat-ed Tommy Gun 6-0," the loudspeaker would blare. "Mr. James won every single point in the match, win-ning his bet with Mr. Gun, who has said he will honor his bet and remain out of Mr. James' path for an entire week. . . ."

Even Evan Grant said something to me about it. Evan was the last person in the world I would have expected to notice.

"That was truly memorable," he said as he passed me in the hall.

"What was?" I asked, catching up with him as he walked to his next class.

"Your world championship match with Tommy Gun, of course."

"Oh, you saw it?"

"Nope. Just heard about it. And I saw the marks all over the court."

"The marks?"

"Yeah, Tommy Gun's black boots left black scuff marks all over the court," Evan said, shaking his head.

I groaned. I'd forgotten that Tommy Gun hadn't played with tennis shoes on. "The court's probably a mess, isn't it?"

"It's in pretty bad shape," Evan said. "I saw maintenance out there this morning trying to take the scuff marks off. They weren't having a whole lot of luck. They'll probably have to repaint the court."

Evan and I, by the way, were headed for another confrontation. I wasn't going to be denied this year. I was going to play on Roosevelt's tennis team, which had fallen short last year in its quest for a state championship. They needed one more good player to make it over the top.

I figured the best thing the tennis coach could do was make Evan and me cocaptains and alternate us in the top spot on the team. That was the easiest thing to do. Evan and I were so closely matched. Sometimes he won when we practiced, and sometimes I won.

And, I figured, as a doubles team, we'd be unbeatable. At least that's what Uncle Teddy said. There was no way anyone would stay with us. I hadn't talked to Evan about the possibility, but he'd surely see the logic.

I didn't see Tommy Gun or any of his pals in the halls on Monday. They were strangely absent. I figured they were hanging out in the boys restroom.

Somebody told me after fifth period, though, that Tommy Gun had skipped school that day. They'd seen his gang riding their bikes around some of the dunes a mile away from the school grounds during lunch.

That was just fine with me. I hoped Tommy Gun stayed out of my way permanently. I had nothing in common with him. I wanted nothing to do with him, if I could help it.

After school, I could have sworn I caught a glimpse of Tommy Gun's gang riding around in the woods near our house. But maybe I was wrong. He didn't know where I lived. At least, I didn't think he did. And what would he want, anyway? What could he do?

I dropped by Karen and Jana's room that night, just to talk. Since coming back from Birmingham and her brief stay with Dad, Karen had been pretty quiet. She'd spent a lot of time by herself. We'd left her alone, and hadn't pressed her much.

But I just sort of figured that enough was enough. It was time Karen came back into the family, all the way back.

Dad, by the way, had gone into a "de-tox" program in Birmingham, Mom told us. He really was trying to stop drinking so much all the time, she said. Time would tell whether it would work or not.

"Whatcha doin'?" I asked Karen from the doorway to her room.

Karen was stretched out on her bed, staring dully at an opened book in front of her. It was obvious she wasn't really studying. She was just hanging out, going through the motions.

"Trying to figure out who won the Civil War," she said, nodding toward the open pages of her book.

"I think the North won," I said.

"The South had better generals," Karen said.

"The North had more men and more equipment."

"But the South had a cause. They were fighting for something."

"Yeah? What were they fighting for?"

"Beats me," Karen laughed. "I still can't figure it out. I don't think they liked Abraham Lincoln's Emancipation Proclamation much."

"Prob'ly not."

"Hey, Cally?" Karen asked, not turning to look at me.

"Yeah?"

"I, um, I never really said thanks."

"For what?"

"You know . . . "

"You mean for coming down to Birmingham with Mom?"

"Yeah, for that."

"Ah, don't sweat it. We all hope Dad gets his life back together. That's all you were hopin' for too."

"I just thought, you know, that maybe I could help . . . "

"I know, Karen. Mom knows too. You just wanted to make it work out. But sometimes things like that just don't work out."

"I think I see that now."

"God has a plan and a time for everything," I said quietly.

"I know that too," Karen said, still not looking around at me.

"You do?"

"Sure. I've heard you and Mom talking. I think I know what's goin' on."

I didn't say anything right away. I'd never heard Karen talk about the Bible or Jesus Christ. But it didn't surprise me that she'd been paying attention to some of the things Mom and I—and sometimes Chris now—talked about. Unlike me, she was pretty good at sorting things out on her own.

"You should read the Bible, one of the Gospels," I

said finally. "Maybe Matthew. It's a really interesting story. You'll like it."

"Maybe I will," she answered. "Maybe I just will."

"Great."

Karen closed her book, and sat up on the bed. "Hey, Cally, you know that guy Tommy Gun?"

I grimaced. "Slightly. What about him?"

"Jana's run into him a couple of times."

My blood froze. I could hear my breathing. I could hear Karen's clock going *ticktock, ticktock.* I could hear the other kids jabbering down in the family room.

"Whatcha mean, Jana's run into him?" I demanded, perhaps a little too harshly. It was hard, sometimes, to remember that Karen was just Jana's sister, not her keeper.

"I mean, she's hung out with Tommy Gun's gang a couple of times."

"You've gotta be kidding?"

"Nope. But, um, Jana was just sort of foolin' around, really," Karen said, trying to rally to her sister's defense. "She wasn't doin' much."

"You don't mess around with a guy like Tommy Gun," I said ominously. "That guy's trouble. Big trouble."

"I know. I'm not blind," Karen said uneasily. "But what can I do about it? You know the way Jana is. She has a mind of her own. And she does crazy things sometimes."

"Well, that's *really* crazy. She should stay as far away from Tommy Gun as she can get."

"Which is exactly why she goes right toward him," Karen said, looking at me. "She's got this little radar that sends her right into trouble. She always has."

"I know," I sighed. "It's the weirdest thing I've ever seen."

"So are you gonna watch out for her?"

"Are you?"

"Sure," Karen shrugged. "But I don't know if there's much I can do. Jana does what she wants to, whether I think it's a good idea or not."

"Well, I'll keep an eye out too. But there's not much I can do, either."

"Well, maybe between the two of us, we can keep her out of trouble," Karen said.

"Maybe. We'll see. Hey, Karen?"

"Yeah?"

"I'm glad you're back," I said, still standing in the doorway to her room.

"Me too," she said, looking away again.

"We all missed you."

"I missed you guys too."

We didn't say anything for a few seconds. But the silence wasn't awkward this time. It was kind of nice.

"Tell me who wins, okay?" I said.

"The South ought to," Karen said, reopening her book. "But somehow I don't think it works out that way."

"That's life," I said.

"Yeah, I know," she answered.

I heard the pebble hit the window. It wasn't real loud. Just a tiny, little *plink* as the rock bounced off the pane of glass that looked out from our loft.

Then I heard it again. *Plink* went the rock. It clattered down the side of our "barn" and landed somewhere on the ground below. I sat bolt upright in bed, listening hard.

"Chris!" I hissed after the third rock had ricocheted off our window.

"What?" came this muffled voice from deep within the covers below me. I never will understand how Chris can sleep like that, with heavy covers piled on top of him.

"There's somebody outside our window," I said, more quietly now.

"No, there isn't," he moaned. "Go back to sleep."

Another rock went *plink* and fell away. "See? Did you hear that?" I asked.

"You're crazy, Cally," Chris said. "Go back to sleep."

I heard Chris roll back the covers, though. I knew he'd popped his head out, just to make sure nothing was going on.

When another rock just missed our window, hitting the side of the house instead, Chris suddenly bolted from his bed and flung the window open. I hopped down from the top of the bunk bed quickly and hurried to the window as well.

"Hey, you!" Chris yelled, his voice sounding very loud in the stillness of the night.

Several dark figures, gathered beneath one of the trees below, suddenly scattered in different directions. It was impossible to tell who they were in the darkness.

"Get outta here!" I yelled.

"Yeah, and don't come back!" Chris added.

One of the fleeing, rock-throwing hoods stopped for a moment. I could just barely see his silhouette as he turned to face our window. For an instant, I thought that maybe it was a girl. I could have sworn I saw her long, flowing hair blowing in the cool, night air.

"Sweet dreams!" this kid yelled, his voice cracking slightly. He was trying to mask his voice by throwing it an octave lower.

I pulled back from the window and began to search the bedroom frantically. I spotted my shoes sticking out from under Chris' bed. I grabbed them and began to yank them on, still standing.

"Hold him here as long as you can," I whispered fiercely to Chris.

"What are ya doin'?" he whispered back.

"I'm goin' out there after them," I said. "Try to keep that one kid talkin'."

"How?"

"I dunno. Just keep talkin' to him."

Chris shrugged, and turned back toward the outside. "Hey, you!" he bellowed toward the kid, who hadn't moved in the few seconds that had just passed. "I'm gonna give your name to the cops!"

I could hear the kid start to laugh as I headed toward the stairs. I could just barely hear him answer that Chris didn't have a clue who he was as I took the stairs three at a time.

I didn't fool around. I pulled the front door of our house open hard, letting it slam back against the closet door in our front hall, and tore out the door. I ran straight for the tree where we'd seen the kids.

Pandemonium broke out. Some of the kids had just been hanging out on their bikes near the street, apparently waiting for their "leader" to join them. Their leader, though, was still on foot, looking up at Chris.

The kids on the bikes started yelling and tearing through the yard on their bikes. One of them came straight at me. I took a swipe at him as he swept by, and missed by a few inches. The kid almost careened into a tree, and only swerved away at the last instant.

Their leader, meanwhile, had recovered his wits in the nick of time. He turned and ran away, his arms flailing in all directions. I sprinted after him.

I almost caught him. I missed by probably a couple of seconds. The kid slid into his bike, almost certainly taking some of the skin off of an arm as he slid across the gravel in our driveway. He got his bike upright, though, and began to peddle away furiously.

I tried to catch him, but the darkness and a ditch that ran along the street near the road kept me from making a straight run at him. Plus, this kid had enough sense to head straight down a steep slope in the road in front of our house. He was already picking up speed when I hit the road.

I ran after him, down the road, for about a hundred yards before giving up. But not before I'd scared the dickens out of him. And not before I'd hurled one last thought at him.

"You won't be so lucky next time!" I called out after the fleeing gang. "I mean it!"

One of the gang members, from somewhere in the darkness, answered my taunt anonymously. "Aw, go suck an egg!" he yelled from a yard somewhere off to my left.

I turned hard left and sprinted in the direction of the voice. There was yet another mad scramble as this second kid put his bike in high gear and tore away from the house. He was gone by the time I arrived at the spot where I thought he'd been.

I stood there, then, breathing hard in the middle of the night, wondering what in blue blazes was going on. This was crazy, absolutely crazy. But, boy, did I feel good. I felt like a knight who'd just successfully defended his castle from marauders.

Well, sort of.

I tried to find Tommy Gun at school the next day. I asked around. Tommy Gun couldn't be found.

I even journeyed back to the boys restroom where I'd first seen him, but the place was empty. There was a faint smell of smoke in the air, but it was a stale smell. Tommy Gun and his gang hadn't been there for a while.

I was pretty sure it was Tommy Gun who'd showed up at our house. It was the only thing that made any sense. But I'd never be able to prove it.

At least they hadn't done any permanent damage. There was no soggy toilet paper strewn around our yard to pick up. They hadn't broken any windows with the little rocks.

I finally stopped thinking about Tommy Gun around fifth period. I had something else on my mind, something that had eaten away at me for almost a year now.

The first day of tennis tryouts began after school. And I wasn't going to make any mistakes this year.

The year before—my first at Roosevelt—I'd made it through the gauntlet. I'd been poised to challenge Evan Grant for the top spot on the team, when I'd made a really dumb mistake.

I'd gotten into a fight during gym class, which led to a three-day suspension. And that prompted the tennis coach to kick me off the team.

No way was I going to do anything *that* dumb this year. I was going to go after Evan with everything I had.

Actually, Evan and I had come a long way in a year. We practiced together a lot at the indoor tennis club. We were almost friends. Almost.

Still, I was about as nervous as I'd ever been as I got dressed in the locker room after school. I was more nervous than I'd been before the national indoor championship match with Evan Grant the year before. There, I'd had nothing to lose. No one was expecting much of me.

But now it was different. I expected to do well. So did kids at school who followed tennis. Failure would mean something, now.

"Not nervous, are you, Cally?" a familiar voice called out to me across the locker room.

"You kiddin'?" I told Evan Grant. "No way."

"Not even a little?" he pressed.

"Piece o' cake," I answered, fumbling with the button on my shirt. I almost tore it off trying to force it through the little hole.

"If you say so," Evan said with a wry smile. "But if your knees were knocking any more, you wouldn't be able to walk."

I just glared at Evan. He did this kind of thing to me all the time. He loved to ride me, give me a hard time before we stepped out on the tennis court. It was psychological war. He really got a kick out of it.

I never tried that stuff. I usually kept my mouth shut and let my racket do all my talking, as they say. I wasn't a genius with words, the way Evan was, so I was better off with the silent route anyway.

When I finally got to the court and started to warm

up, I started to feel better. Once the matches got under way, I knew I'd lose my nervousness. I was pretty sure of that. Everything would be fine.

Tryouts this year would be a little different than they had been the year before. Last year, nearly the entire team was returning, so the tennis coach let the newcomers challenge the varsity for spots on the ten-man roster.

This year, however, five of the varsity had graduated to senior high. The coach decided to let both the returning varsity as well as the challengers play in a round robin tournament. The trick to making the team was to win as many matches as you could during the "tournament."

I drew a seventh-grader during my first match. I'd never seen or heard of him before, but he sure knew who I was.

During warm-ups, he tried to hit the ball back to me as hard as he could. He sprayed quite a few of his shots either wide or long during the warm-up. I couldn't help but smile. There was no way he'd hit like that during the actual match. It never worked out that way.

I was just starting to hit my groove when I heard that crummy voice, the slightly nasal whine I was beginning to recognize.

"Cally James ain't so good," Tommy Gun said from almost directly behind me.   I hit my shot back, and then turned to glance over my shoulder. Tommy Gun was standing at the fence, a few of his gang flanking him on either side. He was smiling broadly.

I didn't say anything. I turned back to my task at hand, but there was a sickening knot starting to grow in my stomach. I wanted with all my might to walk over to the fence and say something to Tommy Gun.

But I knew that would only make it worse.

When I hit one of my warm-up shots wide, the voice kicked into high gear again.

"Yeah! That's more like it!" Tommy Gun called out loudly.

I didn't answer again. I could feel those eyes boring into my back, but I didn't turn around again.

Something hit the back of my head. A small pebble skittled across the tennis court at my feet a moment later.

I whirled, then. "Stop that!" I yelled at Tommy Gun.

"Stop what, dude?" said Tommy Gun, spreading his arms in mock innocence.

That's when I noticed the long, jagged scrape on one of Tommy Gun's forearms. It was just starting to heal. It looked like he'd recently taken a pretty bad fall. Like he'd scraped it across the gravel in someone's driveway sliding into his bike.

"Stop throwing things on the court," I said through clenched teeth.

"So who's doing that?" he asked.

"You are," I said. "Don't do it again."

"Yeah, and whatcha gonna do about it, huh?"

"Just cut it out. I mean it."

"Oooohhh," Tommy Gun said. "He's bad. He's tough."

"Why don't you just leave?" I asked.

"My week's up," said Tommy Gun. "I stayed outta your hair, like I promised. But, dude, now I'm your worst nightmare."

I turned back to the court, where my opponent was waiting patiently. This was going to be a mess. I could see that. But I didn't know what to do. There seemed no end to it.

We finished our warm-ups without another incident,

other than a few shouts and comments. I tried my best to ignore them.

When the actual match began, though, it got a whole lot worse. Tommy Gun, or one of his gang, started to yell on every shot. Then they began to razz me *during* the points.

And, as much as I tried to ignore it, it was starting to get to me. Especially when they'd yell at me right before I'd strike the ball. I started to hit a few balls wide or long.

Even changing sides didn't help, because Tommy Gun and his gang just changed sides with me. They were on a mission, and they were succeeding.

Fortunately, there wasn't much they could do to me when I served. I always hit a hard first or second serve and followed it to the net. From there, the point usually ended quickly, mostly in my direction. So it was pretty easy to win my own service games.

But returning the serve was harder. That's where the razzing was affecting me.

It was painful, but I managed to win the set 6-3. It should have been a blowout. But I was happy to walk away with just a victory, under the circumstances.

After the match was over, I started to walk over to where Tommy Gun and his gang were sitting. I didn't have anything special in mind. I just wanted to do *something*.

Evan Grant intercepted me. "Don't," he said to me quietly, moving to match my pace across the court.

"They're morons," I answered.

"Yeah, we both know that," he said. "But do you want to get kicked off the team for fighting again?"

I stopped and looked at Evan. I almost started laughing. The year before, Evan had been the one who'd gotten another kid to pick a fight with me—just so I *would* get kicked off the team. A lot had happened since then, but we would both never forget that.

"So, this year, you're trying to keep me *out* of a fight?" I said.

Evan laughed lightly. "Hey, what can I say? We need you this year."

"You needed me last year."

"I know. Don't rub it in, okay?"

I glanced over at Tommy Gun, who was still hanging out in the bleachers. "So I shouldn't go rearrange his face?" I said.

"Nah, the guy's a loser. It isn't worth it."

"But he about drove me nuts."

"I know. I could see that," Evan said evenly. "But if you go do something, he'll only come back for more tomorrow."

I sighed. Boy, was this hard. But Evan was right. The best thing to do, by far, was to just turn the other cheek. It hurt, but it had to be the right thing to do.

One of my mom's Bible verses came to mind. Actually, it wasn't *Mom's* verse—they belong to all of us— but I still thought of them as hers because she always pointed them out to me.

Jesus said you should not resist someone who is evil. And if someone hits you on one cheek, turn the other one toward him. What's worse is that Jesus even told us we should love our enemies and pray for them.

I glanced over at Tommy Gun, who was sort of prancing around with his pals just outside the court. How in the world was I supposed to love a guy like him? No way. It was an impossible task.

Yet I could almost hear my mom in the background. "You must try, Cally," she would say. "You must give it your best effort."

It was kind of like eating peas. I hated those crummy things, the way they rolled around in your mouth and then squished when you bit them. But you had to try to eat them. You just knew the rotten things were good for you.

Too bad Mom wasn't around to help me, like she did with the peas. She was tricky, you see. She got you to do what was right, without much of a fuss.

With peas, she'd give us one chance to try and put all of them on our knife. If even one fell off, we had to eat all of them. And we only got one chance to put all of them on the knife. Funny, how I don't *ever* remember putting all the peas on the knife.

But Mom wasn't around to make my choices for me here. I was on my own. I'd rise or fall on my own decisions.

"All right," I sighed to Evan. "I'll leave the guy alone."

"Good," Evan smiled.

"But what I'd really like to do is take that ponytail of his, pull it through the fence, and—

"Don't even think about it," Evan warned. "It'll just make you crazy."

"I think I'm already there."

"It'll pass," Evan promised.

Evan was usually right on the mark. But, somehow, I didn't think he was quite right on this one.

I should have known. Jana doesn't go out of her way to ask me about things unless she has something on her mind. So I should have known. Something should have clicked in the back of my mind.

Three days after the incident on the tennis court, Jana first asked me about Tommy Gun. She was just curious, she said. It was all over school, she said. *Everybody* knew about this war between Tommy Gun and me. Everybody was talking about it. In every hallway corner, in between every class break, kids were *talking,* she said.

Somehow, I doubted that. Maybe Jana and a few of her new friends were talking about it. But I sincerely doubted that it was such a widespread topic of conversation at Roosevelt. Surely, they had better things to talk about.

I was glad of one thing, though. Tommy Gun had grown bored of his game at the tennis court after the second day. When I didn't react to his razzing—and when I'd won my second and third matches without much difficulty—he'd quit coming around.

It was only a moment too soon. Despite my best effort, I think I would have exploded if he'd kept it up. Tommy Gun would never know how close he'd come. He gave up right when he had me where he wanted me.

But I knew Tommy Gun wouldn't give up altogether. He obviously had something else in mind. I just couldn't figure what it might be.

"But why do you have it in for him?" Jana asked me at dinner on that third night.

"I *don't* have it in for him," I said grumpily, wishing we weren't ruining our dinner by talking about the guy.

"Jana, the guy's a big jerk," Chris said, jumping to my defense.

"Maybe *you* just don't know him very well," Jana said to Chris.

"I know a jerk when I see one," Chris fired back.

"How would you know? You've probably never talked to him," Jana said.

"I don't need to," Chris sneered. "You can just tell the guy's a big-time loser."

"Maybe you're the loser," Jana said, her face flushed a little. "And, anyway, there's no way you could know about him. You don't even go to the same school—"

"But I do," I said quickly, before Chris and Jana squared off. "And Chris is right. He's a big jerk."

Mom tried to step in. "Do we really *need* to have this conversation?" she asked, glancing back and forth between Jana and me.

"Jana started it," I protested.

"I didn't," Jana said. "I just asked a question, and Chris—"

"I don't really care who started it," Mom said quickly, staring all of us down. I shrugged, Chris gritted his teeth, and Jana looked away. Argument ended.

"That's better," Mom continued. "Now, can we try something a little more productive? Susan, dear, you haven't told me what happened today at school."

"I wanna hear about the fight between Tommy Gun and Cally," Susan said.

"There hasn't been a fight," Mom said.

"But I'll betcha there will be," Susan chirped, a bright smile on her face. "And Cally'll kill him, I bet."

"Susan! Enough of that," Mom said sharply. "Did you go to school today?"

" 'Course she did," John said.

"And what happened?" Mom asked, looking at Susan.

"Same old stuff," Susan said.

"Okay, why don't you tell us about it," Mom insisted.

"It's just readin' books, and writin' letters, and all of that," Susan said. Clearly, she wanted to know more about Tommy Gun.

"Susan, dear, I think we'd all love to hear about what you did at school today," Mom said.

"Oh, all right," Susan sighed. "Well, this one girl spilled the watercolors all over her dress, and she had to go home for the day. And then Benjamin—he's this boy who always tries to chase me around at recess— well, he . . . "

*　*　*　*　*

Jana found me later that night. She just couldn't let it rest. She was bound and determined to discover why I had it in for Tommy Gun.

"Give it up, Jana," I pleaded with her. "Please. I don't have it in for the guy. He's the one who's made my life miserable, not the other way around."

Jana had cornered me in the loft, while I was trying to study. Actually, I didn't mind the interruption. I was reading this deadly dull story about some German mythological character—Lorelei, a siren along the Rhine whose beautiful singing lured the sailors to shipwreck—and it was really putting me to sleep.

I looked up from my mythology book and studied my sister for a second, sort of ignoring what she was saying. Jana was a lot like this Lorelei character. She was a real heartbreaker. Good thing Mom wouldn't let her date yet. Things would really be messy when *that* started.

"Cally, are you listening to me?" Jana demanded.

"Um, sure."

"No, you're not. You haven't heard a word I've said."

"Sure I have. You were talking about that jerk, Tommy Gun."

"But he's *not* a jerk."

I paused, not sure I should tell Jana about the other night. But she needed to know. "Jana, I'm pretty sure it was Tommy Gun who was over here the other night," I said finally.

"Over where?"

"Here. At our house."

Her eyes narrowed suspiciously. "What was he doing here?"

"He was throwing rocks at our house, for one thing."

"Throwing rocks?"

"Well, actually, he was throwing them at our window. At Chris' and mine, I mean."

"How do you know?"

"We heard the rocks hit the window, and—"

"No, no," she said quickly. "How do you know it was Tommy Gun who did it?"

" 'Cause I chased them away. I ran after them. And one of them, their leader, slid across the gravel in our driveway as he tried to get to his bike."

"So what?" Jana said testily.

"So I saw Tommy Gun with this long scrape on his

arm the next day. Just like he'd slid across some gravel."

"That doesn't prove anything," Jana said with a frown. "Maybe he got in a fight—"

"Yeah, and maybe he fell in our driveway as I was chasing him away," I said softly, gazing hard at my younger sister. What was going on here? Why was she so keen on defending Tommy Gun? Was I just not understanding? Was I missing something?

"You don't know that, Cally. And, anyway, there aren't any broken windows. So it wasn't really all that bad or anything."

I turned around all the way in my chair. "Hey, Jana, are you hangin' out with Tommy Gun or somethin'? You seem so interested in this guy—"

"No, I'm not," Jana answered, shaking her long, black hair emphatically. "I've talked to him a couple of times. That's all."

"And he seems all right to you?"

She smiled shyly. "He's funny. He makes me laugh."

My eyes opened wide. "He's funny?"

"Sure. He always cuts up about all the teachers at Roosevelt. It's really funny."

"I'll bet," I said sarcastically.

"He's not bad, Cally," Jana insisted. "He's just, um, different. That's all."

"Jana, for cryin' out loud, he hangs out in the boys restroom and smokes," I said, growing thoroughly exasperated with Jana's absolute refusal to see things the way they were. All right, maybe it was the way I saw it. But was there any real doubt about what a loser Tommy Gun was?

"*Lots* of kids smoke," she said.

"Yeah, and lots of kids are stupid," I said angrily. "Smoking's about the dumbest thing imaginable. It wrecks your lungs. I couldn't finish off a tennis match if I smoked."

"I dunno. I think it seems pretty cool," Jana said casually.

I gripped the chair hard, mostly to keep from catapulting from it in Jana's direction. "Cool?" I asked in a tight voice instead. "You haven't tried it, have you?"

Jana looked at me with those innocent eyes of hers, probably calculating if she could trust me or not. I was sure Karen knew the answer to that question. But Karen would never tell a soul. That's why Jana trusted her completely.

"Maybe I have, maybe I haven't," she said evasively. "And, anyway, it's none of *your* business."

"You're crazy if you smoke. I mean it, Jana. It isn't cool. Look at what it did to Great-grandpa . . . "

"Ah, he was just really old."

"He wasn't *that* old, Jana. He was 58 when he died from that lung cancer stuff. And you know how much Great-grandpa smoked."

"That's really old, Cally," Jana said confidently. "And, brother, nobody I know's gonna smoke like that all their life, like Great-grandpa did. Everybody I know's gonna stop after awhile."

"After it's no longer cool, you mean?"

"Yeah, maybe. Or when you get to college, or leave home. Like that."

This was easily one of the dumbest conversations I'd ever had with Jana. I mean, one of the all-time winners. You had to be a complete, utter moron to smoke. You had to have cobwebs for brains to try cigarettes. It wasn't cool, I wanted to tell her. It was just plain dumb.

But I knew Jana would never listen to me. She never did. In fact, if I told her one thing, she was liable to do just the opposite. So if I said smoking was dumb and moronic and something only twit-brains did, she was as likely to go out and buy a pack as do anything else.

"Jana, I have to get back to my studies," I said. "Lorelei calls."

"Who?"

"Never mind. It's a private joke."

"Oh. Well, um, you know, I just wanted to tell you that Tommy Gun isn't really all that bad. That's why I came up here . . ."

I shook my head sadly. "Jana, you're never gonna change my mind. Tommy Gun's trouble. Big trouble. If I were you I'd just stay out of his way."

"Well, you're *not* me," Jana said, edging back toward the door. "And I'll do whatever I want. Just 'cause you're older than me doesn't mean you can tell me what kind of friends I can have."

"Jana, I'm not tryin'—"

But Jana had already vanished. I thought briefly about following her, to tell her that I really didn't want to run her life or anything like that. But it wouldn't do any good. Like I said, Jana never listens to me. Not ever.

Elaine Cimons cornered me in the hallway again. I hate that. She always does it to me. I'll just be walking along, minding my own business, and she'll find me, pin me up against the wall, and make my life miserable.

Actually, she doesn't make my life miserable. She just makes me *feel* lousy because I hadn't read the latest chapter for our Bible study—which was still going on, even though summer vacation had ended—or I was thinking about something Christians shouldn't really think about or because I was about to do something I really shouldn't do.

"Come on, Cally, let's go," she said over my shoulder as I was gazing stupidly at the haphazard contents of my locker.

I sort of jerked around at the sound of her voice. Elaine had that kind of effect on me. I always jumped when she first said something to me. "What for?" I asked, my voice raspy. "Where are we going?"

"The principal's office," she said rather definitively.

I just *knew* this was trouble. Nobody, but nobody, goes to the principal's office on their own. You're either dragged there kicking and screaming or you meet your parents there for some crummy reason or your teacher sends you there because you've tried to set a girl's hair on fire.

"Why? I don't want to go to the principal's office," I objected.

"Yes, you do," she said. "You're going with me."

"But why? What are you gonna do there?"

"We're going to see the principal, of course."

"We are?"

"Sure we are."

"And then what?"

"Then we're going to tell him about the club we want to form after school."

"What club?"

"The Bible club," she said. Her eyes had that glow in them again. Now I really knew we were headed into a storm. I just knew it.

"What's a Bible club?" I asked.

"A club that meets to study parts of the Bible, you silly," she giggled. "What'd you think it was?"

"Beats me," I shrugged. "It's your idea."

"Well, I figured, seeing as how they have chess clubs and drama clubs, why not a Bible club?"

"I don't know, Elaine," I said cautiously. "I don't think they'll let us do something like this. Isn't there some law that says you can't do something like that in a public school?"

"Not anymore there isn't," Elaine said confidently.

"You sure?"

"Yes, I'm sure," she said. "Now, let's go."

I sighed. This was not going to be any fun. I was sure of that. But I couldn't say no to Elaine. I hadn't been able to right from the moment she first bumped into me in the hallway the year before.

We trudged through the halls and walked into the principal's office. Elaine had that swagger to her walk, which meant she was on a mission. She was *not* going to be denied.

"I'm sorry, but the principal does not see students without an appointment," the secretary said.

"Okay, we'll come back," I said sheepishly, edging toward the door.

"No, we won't," Elaine said fervently. "Please, can't we see him for just a minute? It won't take very long."

"I'll be glad to put you down on his calendar," the secretary offered. "I think I can probably fit you in next week sometime."

"Please, can't we just see him for one second right now," Elaine pressed. "I promise it won't take long."

"No, I really think it would be better if you scheduled an—"

The door to the principal's office swung open. John Kamber poked his head out, looking first at his secretary and then at Elaine and me.

"Is there a problem?" Kamber asked.

"There's no problem," his secretary said. "I was just putting these two young people on your calendar."

"Please, Mr. Kamber, can't we see you just for a second?" Elaine asked, not wanting to lose the opportunity.

"Well, Miss, I'm rather busy at the moment—"

"It won't take long. I promise." Elaine edged a step closer to Kamber's office. I didn't budge.

Kamber paused, then smiled rather bleakly and finally nodded at Elaine, who didn't waste a second and almost marched right into his office. She didn't even glance at his secretary on her way in.

"Thank you," I said to Kamber's secretary.

"You're quite welcome, young man," she answered. "In the future, perhaps you can convince your friend to schedule an appointment first?"

"I'll try," I sighed. "But Elaine sort of does what she wants."

"I can see that," his secretary said dryly.

I followed Elaine into the inner sanctum. The last time I'd been here was with Mom, on my first day of school more than a year ago. That hadn't been a whole lot of fun.

"Well, well," Kamber said, lifting one knee over the edge of his desk as he sort of half-sat, half-leaned against it. "Cally James. You still go by Cally, do you? You haven't decided to go with the name your parents gave you at birth?"

"Yes, sir, it's still Cally," I said tightly. I liked my name just fine the way it was.

"Well, someday you'll really want to change it back. You can't go through life as Cally."

"I like my name just fine, sir," I said firmly.

"Mr. Kamber, we'd like to ask you permission to do something," Elaine said quickly, changing the subject. For once, I was glad she'd jumped in.

"And what might that be?" Kamber asked light-heartedly.

"We want to form a Bible club," she said.

"On the school grounds?" Kamber asked, his eyes opening ever so slightly in surprise.

"Yes, on the school grounds," Elaine answered.

Kamber's jaw muscles tightened and began to work themselves back and forth as he thought about it. I could only imagine what might be going through his mind.

"I don't think so," he said finally. "I just can't allow it."

"But why not?" Elaine demanded. It was curious, but she didn't seem disappointed by his decision. She seemed invigorated, somehow.

"Well, for one thing, I'm relatively certain there's a state law that does not permit that sort of an activity on the grounds of a public school."

"Mr. Kamber, there was a Supreme Court decision
that said just this kind of a club was allowed in a
public school," Elaine said emphatically. She was
clearly prepared for this. I wondered how long she'd
been plotting this.

Kamber pursed his lips in thought. "Well, yes, I believe you're right about that," he said slowly. "I do
recall that Supreme Court ruling. But I'm not sure it
applies here. I'll have to look into it."

"So you'll let us know?" Elaine said brightly. The
door had opened just a crack. If I knew Elaine, she
wouldn't stop until she'd burst right through it.

"Yes, I'll let you know of my final decision. It may
take a few weeks. Can you wait?"

"We'll wait," Elaine said, nodding.

"Good, then if you'll excuse me," Kamber said, dis-
missing us. "I've got a stack of work awaiting me."

We left quickly, Elaine marching out as she'd
marched in. Boy, was she a tornado. I felt an awful lot
like Dorothy's house, which got sucked up in one of
those twisters. But at least Dorothy's tornado set her
down in Oz. I had no idea where Elaine the tornado
was likely to send me.

I started to get nervous when I didn't see Tommy Gun for almost an entire week. He was around, I guess. But he didn't go out of his way to find me, and I wasn't about to go looking for him. I should have known it was too good to be true, though.

Chris and I were studying in the family room when we heard it. Actually, neither of us was studying. Or, at least, we weren't studying real well.

It was Monday night, and we were paying a whole lot more attention to the second quarter of the football game between the Washington Redskins and the Atlanta Falcons than we were to our books.

It was funny. I'd lived in Washington for a year now, and I still hadn't figured out how to become a Redskins fan. I couldn't help it. I still liked the Falcons, like just about everybody else in the Deep South west of Florida and east of Louisiana.

Chris, though, had already adapted. He was a rabid Redskins fan. Which made for some pretty loud shouting matches on Sunday, when they play most of the pro games.

"Get rid of the ball!" Chris yelled at the screen. "Get rid of it, you ... "

The Redskins quarterback didn't get rid of the ball, and he was sacked for about an eight-yard loss, deep in the Redskins territory.

"Yes!" I cheered. "The Redskins have *no* pass defense. None. Their line is like a sieve."

"Yeah, well, the Falcons are about as slow as water buffaloes," Chris fired back. "The only reason they got to him was that the stupid quarterback held onto the ball too long. He had plenty of time to get rid of it."

"The secondary had the receivers covered like a blanket," I gloated. "He didn't have anybody to throw to."

"Oh, gimme a break," Chris sneered. "The Falcons' secondary is a joke. Usually, they give up about a hundred points through the air."

"They aren't tonight, are they?" I smirked.

The Redskins hadn't gotten untracked yet, and the Falcons were up by two touchdowns already. So it was safe to puff up my chest a little. Atlanta was in control.

"A bomb, a bomb!" Chris yelled at the screen. "Go for it!"

The Redskins' quarterback unloaded the ball, deep. It sailed about 50 yards, into the Falcons' territory. One of the Redskins' all-pro receivers pulled it down. The Falcons' secondary caught him and tackled him, but not until he'd taken the ball inside their 20-yard-line.

"Seventy yards!" Chris said, raising both hands high and knocking his books off his lap in the process. Papers, pencil, and books all tumbled to the floor. Chris didn't even glance down.

"Brother, was that ever lucky," I muttered.

"Luck? Are you nuts? That was a perfectly thrown pass."

"Come on. The guy was in the right place at the right time—"

"Yeah, past the Falcons' secondary, that's where."

"A zone defense. Their coverage must have gotten mixed up somehow," I said, coming to my team's defense.

Chris was ignoring me again. One of Washington's other all-pro receivers was running a slant, toward the end zone. Their quarterback laid the ball in perfectly, just beyond the reach of one of the Falcons' corner-backs. Just like that, they'd cut the Falcons' "insur-mountable" lead nearly in half.

"Touchdown!" Chris yelled at the top of his lungs, jumping out of his chair. He started to do a victory dance around the family room.

"Sit down," I growled.

Chris paid me no attention. He aimed his victory dance slightly in my direction. When he was close enough, I reached out with my hand—spilling all of *my* books onto the floor—and grabbed his T-shirt. Chris jerked free and continued his prancing.

"Touch-down, touch-down," he started to chant.

"Would you sit down and shut up already," I said.

"Eighty-five yards in 30 seconds," Chris said. "That's some defense the Falcons have."

"They're still leading," I said lamely.

"Not for long," Chris answered.

Just then, a lightning bolt hit one of the trees right outside our window. *Whomp-Boom!* I bolted out of my chair, and Chris whirled around toward the window that looked out on our front yard.

"Man, that was close," Chris said.

I hurried to the door. That was no lightning bolt. There hadn't been a cloud in the sky when Chris and I had come in after dinner. And it wasn't raining out-side now.

"Where're you goin'?" Chris asked.

"To see what that was."

"It was just lightning."

"I don't think so," I called out over one shoulder.

When I got outside, I glanced up at the night sky. About a thousand million stars winked back at me. So that had not been lightning.

Then I saw the orange glow through the trees, out toward the road. I trotted across the front lawn. Our front door opened again, and Chris hurried out after me.

I got to it a few seconds before Chris did. Once upon a time, it had been our mailbox. Now, it was just a flattened, charbroiled heap on the side of the road. The post it had rested on was bent to one side, the end of it shredded and mangled.

"Whoa!" Chris muttered when he reached my side. "That's some major damage."

"Slightly," I said angrily.

"Blew it to smithereens," Chris marveled.

I didn't answer. I was scouring the landscape for something, some clue. All I found was the remnants of what had once been a copper pipe. I reached down and touched it. The thing was white hot.

"Whatcha got?" Chris asked, looking over my shoulder.

"A pipe bomb," I said. "That's what it was."

"What's that?"

"It's easy to make," I answered. "I knew a kid once who made 'em. You take a copper pipe, fill it up with gunpowder, stick a fuse in it, and there you are. A homemade bomb."

"Yow!" Chris said, still clearly impressed at how the perpetrators had absolutely, completely knocked our mailbox for a loop.

"Hey, Chris? Can you run in and get a flashlight real quick? And tell Mom what happened?"

"Sure," Chris said quickly, already running toward the house.

I continued to look around the mangled mailbox, but it was hard to see anything in the dark. Chris returned soon, though, with the flashlight. Mom was with him.

"Oh, my," Mom said, covering her mouth.

"It'll be okay, Mom," I said reassuringly. "Chris and I'll go by the hardware store and get another one tomorrow, after school, and put it up. No problem."

"Who would do such a thing?" Mom asked. "This is so ... so vicious. Who would be so angry at us that they would do something like this?"

I shook my head. "Mom, I don't think anybody was angry. It's just a prank. Kids do stuff like this all the time."

"Like this?" Mom asked, incredulous.

"Well, maybe not quite this bad," I confessed.

"I can understand a little toilet paper on the trees, or maybe a tire track in the front yard," Mom said. "But this?"

"Mom, if it's who I think it is, these kids are real punks," I said.

"You think it's Tommy Gun's gang?" Chris asked.

"Who else?" I shrugged.

"Tommy Gun?" Mom asked. "Who's that?"

"You know, that kid at Cally's school, the one we were talking about last week," Chris answered.

I switched the flashlight on and started to sweep the beam back and forth across the ground around the mailbox. I spotted the crisscrossing bicycle tire tracks almost immediately.

"Do you see 'em, Chris?" I asked.

"Yeah, I see 'em," he answered.

"See what?" Mom asked.

I pointed to the tire tracks. There were a whole

bunch of them. They were all tracks of wide-tread tires, like the kind you'd find on souped-up BMX bikes. The kind of bikes Tommy Gun and his gang rode around on.

"It had to be them," I said.

Chris nodded. "No question about it."

Mom folded her arms in disgust. She was angry, now, more than anything else. "So you think you know who might have done this?"

"Yep, I'm pretty sure," I answered.

"Well, I'll fix their wagons," she said, turning toward the house.

"Whatcha gonna do, Mom?" Chris called out after her.

"I'm going to call the FBI, that's what," she said.

"The FBI?" I almost gasped.

"Sure," she called back. "What these kids did is a federal offense, and it's also an act of terrorism. That makes it the FBI's business." Mom vanished into the trees then.

"Holy Cow!" Chris muttered in awe. "The FBI."

"Boy, oh boy, will Tommy Gun squirm when that FBI agent shows up at his door," I said.

"It'll be great, won't it?" Chris grinned.

"Tremendous," I answered.

There would only be one slight problem, of course. Tommy Gun would know who ratted on him. And then he'd *really* come looking for me.

11

The FBI agent showed up at our house the next day and grilled Chris and me. About halfway through, I was beginning to feel like I'd done something wrong, that I was the one who was going on trial.

"So, Mr. James, can you explain to me exactly how you know this Mr. Tommy Gun, and why you suspect him of this felony?" the agent asked me.

The agent's dark sunglasses were tucked neatly inside his suit coat pocket. His intense eyes bored into mine, obviously looking for any sign of weakness, any sign of deceit or malicious intent on my part.

"I, um, I met Tommy Gun in the boys restroom," I answered quite uneasily.

"The boys restroom?"

"Yeah, they were smoking, and I—"

"Smoking is a prohibited activity on the school premises?"

"You can't smoke in school, that's right," I said.

"I see. And you went in there to smoke as well?"

"No, no," I said quickly. "I don't smoke. I went in there because I was, um, well, trying to avoid this person."

"This person?"

"Um, Elaine Cimons. She's this girl, this friend, I have."

"And you were trying to avoid a friend by going into

a restroom where they smoke illegally?"

"I didn't *know* they were smoking in there until I actually got inside," I said defensively.

"I see. So you were running away from a friend—"

"I wasn't running away. I didn't want to see her just then."

"So how long did you interact with this Tommy Gun character?"

"Oh, I was only in there for a few minutes."

"It took that long to do what you had to do?"

"No, we got to talking."

"Talking?"

"Yeah, Tommy Gun and I were talking."

"About anything specific?"

"No, not really. Tennis, mostly."

"Tennis?"

"I play a lot of tennis."

"Anything else? Any other encounters with this Tommy Gun fellow?"

"Cally played him in tennis. Whomped him pretty good," Chris offered.

"You *played* Tommy Gun in tennis?" the agent asked, his eyes slightly raised.

"It was a challenge," I said quickly. "A bet."

"You partook of this illegal gambling wager with Tommy Gun on public property?"

"No, no. There wasn't any money involved," I said, starting to sweat. "It was just a friendly bet."

"I thought you said you were not a friend of this Tommy Gun?"

"Well, no, we aren't. I, um, meant that it was just a bet without money. No money. For other things." This whole thing was really starting to make me nervous. I was beginning to wish Mom hadn't bothered to call the FBI.

"I see. So you met this Tommy Gun and talked about tennis, then you played him in tennis. Anything else?"

"Yeah, he was chucking rocks at our window," Chris blurted.

"Chucking rocks?"

"Some kids threw rocks at our window the other night," I said.

"I see. And you saw Tommy Gun throwing these rocks?"

"Well, um, no, not exactly."

"Not exactly?"

"I saw the scrape on his arm, you see . . ."

"The scrape on his arm?"

"Yeah, I chased the kid who was throwing the rocks down our driveway, and he slid on the gravel. And then I saw Tommy Gun with this long scrape on his arm the next day."

The FBI agent frowned. It was almost a scowl. "That's *very* circumstantial, Mr. James. Very circumstantial. Not much I can do with that bit of information, I'm afraid."

"Well, I just *know* it was Tommy Gun," I said.

"Yes, I'm sure you do. Anything else?"

I thought about it for a moment. Nothing else really came to mind, other than this vague feeling about Tommy Gun and Jana. "Well, you know, he's sort of talked to one of my sisters a couple of times," I mumbled.

"Pardon me?"

"I said he's talked to Jana, my sister," I said more clearly.

"I see. Your sister and this Tommy Gun have had several conversations?"

"Something like that," I muttered.

"I see. Anything else?"

"No, I guess not," I said after another long pause.

The FBI agent sat there, not moving a muscle, just sort of staring at Chris and me. "So let's see if I can sum up, here. You met this Tommy Gun, talked about tennis, played a friendly match with him. You suspect him of throwing a rock at your window, but you can't prove it. And he talks to your sister occasionally. Is that accurate?"

"Yeah, pretty much," I answered.

The agent sighed, shook his head and started to rise from the sofa. "Not much to go on, Mr. James. Not much at all."

"So you're not going to do anything?"

"No, I didn't say that," the agent said. "I may go by and question him. That occasionally has some benefit. But this Tommy Gun character, I'm guessing, won't be intimidated by an interview."

"Waddya mean?" Chris asked.

The agent smiled, for the first time in the interview. "In my years of law enforcement, I've discovered an interesting principle."

"What's that?" I asked.

"The good guys always sweat," he said, grinning. "The really bad ones are always cool as cucumbers."

"You're kidding?"

"Lying's an art, son," the FBI agent said, moving toward our front door. "It takes years of practice. The really bad ones have invested a lifetime in that art, and they're almost always very, very good at it."

"Wow," Chris said.

"That's pretty wild," I marveled. "I never really thought about it like that."

"I know," the FBI agent said. "Most people don't. If they did, it would really make my job hard."

"So you're gonna go by and see Tommy Gun anyway?" I asked.

The agent paused at the doorway. "Yes, I believe I will. Perhaps a little intervention, now, could do wonders for us later."

"What?" I asked.

The agent looked at me. "Another principle I've learned. Once somebody starts to go bad, it almost never turns around. They just keep going on to other things throughout the course of their lives."

"That sounds pretty crummy," I offered.

"Unfortunate, but true," the agent said. "But if you can get to a kid early and turn it around, there's some hope."

I wasn't sure I agreed with the agent. I guess I thought that kids could be kids, and then figure out what it all meant later on. But what did I know? He was the expert.

"I dunno," I volunteered. "It can't *always* work that way."

"Often enough," the agent said. "By the time a kid winds up in a juvenile detention facility, he's well down the road to a life of crime."

I winced. That sounded so bleak, so crummy, so . . . final. A life of crime. It sounded like such a horrible fate.

"I don't think this Tommy Gun's like that," I said. "He's just sort of a punk, that's all. He just likes to be different."

The agent turned to walk away from the house. "For his sake, I hope you're right, Mr. James. I truly do."

Yeah, me too.

I just had a feeling. You know, when your head starts to tingle all over. You just know something's up, that there's something right around the corner.

I was still riding my bike to school. I wouldn't start riding the bus until it got *really* cold outside. I can't stand riding the bus. I'd rather go on my bike.

I rode to school the same way every day. I'd get up some steam down the big hill in front of our house, cut through the gas station at the bottom, ride for about a mile down another street that took me right to some woods at the back of the school grounds, and then peddle furiously through a path in the woods that led to the football locker room.

Usually these days, it was still pretty dark in the woods in the morning. The sun had already come up, barely, but it was almost always chilly and dark in the woods, so I just tried to get through as quickly as I could.

That morning, as I entered the woods, I had that feeling. I just wanted to get through those dark woods as fast as I could. I peddled just a little bit faster, my heart beating just a little harder.

I never even saw the rope stretched out across the path. It was strategically placed in the shadows of a large stand of trees, and I didn't see it until I was right on it.

The front wheel of my bike hit the taut rope and skipped over it. The front of the bike thudded to the ground, hard. The crank got tangled up in the rope then, causing the rear wheel to pitch high in the air.

I'd really been moving, and the sudden jerk as the crank caught the rope tossed me headfirst over the handlebars. I never had a chance to hold on. It all happened in the blink of an eye.

Instinctively, I rolled up into a tuck as I was jerked up into the air. It was funny what you thought about at moments like this. It reminded me of the first time we did forward somersaults over the horse in gym class. You'd run along the mats, catapult up and over the horse, and then do a tuck roll onto the mats on the other side.

That's what I was thinking about as I hurtled through the air. I was thinking about gym class, and landing on the other side of the horse, about how the breath was always knocked out of you a little when you hit the mats.

There really wasn't any time to panic. I barely had enough time to react, go into a tuck and wait for the ground to crunch me. There weren't any nice, soft gym mats out here. Only the cold, hard ground.

The back of my head hit the ground first. I rolled my head forward as I hit, tucking it in against my chest. My legs came whipping around as my back hit the ground with a "thud." My legs hit an instant later with a jolt, the pain shooting up both sides. My breath whooshed out.

Almost immediately, I heard a screech and a yell from behind the trees off to my right. My bike went crashing off into the woods to the left, disappearing into the tall grass. I just lay there on the ground, too stunned to move.

I didn't think anything was broken. But, boy, did my legs ache. So did my back. My head had a knot on it from where it had struck the ground. I just wanted to stay where I was for a while.

"You should'na called the FBI, dude," this voice called out from the shadows of the trees off to my right, in the direction I'd heard the yell as I'd crashed to the ground.

I didn't say anything back. I don't think I could have even if I'd wanted to. I wasn't sure my voice would work.

"That was a mistake, man," a second, higher-pitched voice called out. That had to be Squirrel. The first voice had obviously been Tommy Gun.

"Yeah, dude, it was a *big* mistake," Tommy Gun said. "You're gonna pay for it, big-time."

"Yeah, you're gonna pay," echoed Squirrel.

I still lay there, gulping for air. Each breath hurt a little less as time wore on. I'd be able to get up and limp to school in maybe a few hundred years.

"So why'd you do it?" Tommy Gun asked. I could tell by the sound of his voice that he was about fifteen feet away, maybe a little farther. I couldn't see him, though, because he was behind a tree or something.

I still didn't answer. I was thinking. *What had I gotten myself into? How would I ever get out of this mess I was sinking into? Would this guy ever go away?*

"Come on, why'd you do it?" Tommy Gun demand-ed. "It was no big deal. It was just a stupid mailbox, that's all. Why'd you have to go and call the FBI, for cryin' out loud?"

"I didn't call 'em," I grunted finally. I winced. It *did* hurt to talk.

"Somebody did, dude, and it wasn't no tooth fairy

who done it," Tommy Gun sneered.

"My mom did," I said. "She called the FBI."

I could hear the two of them talking that one over. I couldn't quite hear what they were discussing, though.

"How'd your old lady know about us, though?" Squirrel asked.

"Waddya mean?" I asked.

"How'd she know to finger us?" Tommy Gun asked. "You musta told her."

I closed my eyes. I wondered why they didn't just come out of the shadows of the trees and finish the job. I was helpless here. They could pummel me into oblivion if they wanted to.

"Yeah, sure, I told her I thought it was you," I managed.

"Why'd you do that, you moron?" Squirrel whined. "I thought this was between you and us? Why'd you have to go bringin' the cops in?"

"I didn't bring anybody in," I said. I was starting to get angry now that I was beginning to breathe normally. "You were the idiots who blew up our mailbox. My mom was the one who called the FBI."

"Well, I don't care *who* called the cops," Tommy Gun growled. "This is between us. You don't need no cops to do your stinkin' business."

"For the last time, I didn't call them," I almost yelled.

Tommy Gun started to laugh. It sounded like a wounded hyena, not that I'd ever actually heard one. "I got him, though," he said.

"Got who?" I asked.

"That FBI agent. I had him eatin' outta my hand. He believed every word I said. He never suspected nuthin'." Squirrel started to laugh too. Clearly, something was extraordinarily funny.

I remembered what the agent had told me. The good guys always squirm. The rotten ones can lie through their teeth and get away with it.

"So what're you worried about, then?" I asked.

"Nuthin'," Tommy Gun said. "But you got plenty."

I tried to ease up into a sitting position. I still couldn't think real clearly. My head was throbbing with pain, and my eyes felt a little blurry. "What do you mean?" I grunted.

"You'll be seein' more of me, that's all."

"Yeah? Why?"

"Oh, I dunno. Your sister's kinda takin' a liking to me, for one thing." Tommy Gun chuckled. It sent shivers up my spine.

"Stay away from her," I said through clenched teeth. "I mean it."

"Yeah, and whatcha gonna do about it if I don't?"

"Just stay away from her," I said. "I *mean* it."

"Hey, dude, you never know," Tommy Gun said. "We might be, you know, like, relatives someday." Squirrel started to laugh, his voice squealing like a pig on the butcher's block.

Despite the pain, I rose to my feet, my head complaining loudly with every move. Without even thinking about what I was doing, or why, I charged madly into the forest toward the direction of their voices.

They scattered almost the moment I started to charge after them. They'd been clearly watching me like a hawk, expecting me to come after them. They'd probably already mapped out their escape route.

I crashed into a tree and clutched it for all it was worth. My breath came in gasps. I could hear the sound of feet crashing through the underbrush. They were already well away.

I stayed there for a couple of minutes, holding the tree up. Finally, the world stopped spinning. A few crickets chirped. A bird called out. The wind sent shivers through the leaves above my head.

I ducked my head against the wind and walked back, gingerly, to retrieve my bike. The rope that had tripped me up was still taut across the path. Viciously, I pulled one end free and flung it into the woods.

13

Now, I had a problem. Should I confront Jana? Should I march into her room, demand to know if she was starting to pal around with Tommy Gun? Should I tell her that was a big mistake?

And what if she was hanging around with Tommy Gun? Was that like dating, which Mom had absolutely, positively told Jana she could not do yet? What would I do if she was?

I knew one thing. Or, at least, I'd made up my mind about one thing. For better or worse, I wasn't going to go to Mom anymore about this little problem I now had with Tommy Gun. I didn't want any more trip wires in the dark woods. No more of that.

I knew I'd struggle with this silence, no matter what happened from here on out. I had a feeling it would be a terrible struggle. I'd always told Mom about everything. Now that I'd become a Christian, I felt doubly obliged to be as honest as possible about all things.

But I was really stuck, here. I just didn't know what to do. I didn't want to get Jana in trouble. I was partly to blame for the fact that Tommy Gun was circling around her like a shark. So I'd have to fix it.

In the end, I decided I had to confide in Karen. Maybe she could help me. If I confronted Jana, it would only make it worse. I knew that. She never listened to me. If I said anything to her, I couldn't be sure how she'd react.

"She's talked about him, a little," Karen said as she sort of nibbled on her bagel at lunch at school later that week.

"Just a little?" I asked in between bites. I was wolfing down the turkey sandwich I'd packed and brought with me.

"She's pretty secretive about that kind of stuff these days."

"Even with you?" I asked, a little amazed.

"Even with me," Karen confessed. "There are things we don't always talk about."

It was strange. You live your whole life with your sister, and you still find out things about her you don't know. I thought Jana and Karen talked about *everything* together. But maybe they didn't.

It was also strange to be sitting with Karen at lunch. I think this was the very first time, ever, that we'd actually sat together at lunch. I don't know why we never had before. We just hadn't. It had never been something either of us had wanted to do.

Karen had really given me a strange look when I'd asked her to sit with me too. It was one of those "are-you-out-of-your-mind" looks.

She made us pick out a seat way at one end of the cafeteria, like she was embarrassed to be seen with me or something. I guess it wasn't cool to hang out with your older brother. Oh well.

"But is there some way to find out if she's seeing this guy, Tommy Gun?" I persisted.

Karen shrugged. "I can try, I guess."

"I mean, she does talk about stuff like that every once in awhile, doesn't she?"

"If she feels like it. If she doesn't, she won't."

"Really?"

Karen looked away, out over the rest of the cafeteria. We were well away from most of her friends. They were sitting in bunched groups in the middle of the cafeteria, which was in the smaller, older gym. Karen and I were plastered up against the wall under one of the basketball rims.

"Since I came back from Alabama, Jana's sort of gone her own way," Karen volunteered. She was still looking away.

"Waddya mean?"

Karen looked back at me. There was a quiet plea in her eyes. "We don't talk as much. She's making some of her own friends at school . . ."

"She's always had her own friends," I offered.

"I know, but this is, um, different." Karen hesitated. "We're kind of goin' in different directions. Jana's not paying attention to her homework as much. She's foolin' around more. I can't figure her out like I used to be able to."

I shrugged. "Jana's always done her own thing. She's always gone her own way."

"I know, but she used to tell me about what she was doing. Now, she keeps a lot of stuff to herself."

Like I said, you go your whole life, thinking you know your sister. Then you find out you didn't really know her as well as you thought.

"We'll both keep an eye on her, okay?"

Karen nodded. "Okay."

" 'Cause I'm tellin' you, this guy Tommy Gun's a real jerk."

"I believe you."

Karen looked across the room again, like she was nervous or something. "Can I, um, go sit with my friends now? Is it okay?"

I laughed. "Yeah, sure. That's all I wanted to talk about."

"You sure? I mean, it's not like I don't like you or anything like that."

"It's all right. Don't worry about it."

A look of relief came over her. "It's just that my friends are *looking* at me—"

"Karen, I said it was all right," I said, shaking my head. "Get outta here. Move!"

Karen bolted from her seat like she'd been shot out of a cannon. All she had with her was a bagel and a Diet Coke. I never know how she survives on that, but somehow she manages.

I watched her walk quickly across the cafeteria. When she got to the knot of friends who always sat together during lunch, they all swarmed around her, closing her in, when she sat down. One or two of her friends kept glancing over their shoulders, taking covert peeks at me.

It sure was funny. I saw Karen every day, at breakfast and dinner. We goofed around together all the time at home. We did things together. We were pretty tight, all things considered.

But she didn't want to be caught dead hanging around me at school. It was positively weird. I couldn't figure it out to save my life. It was like I had some disease or something. Maybe I'd figure it out someday.

Then again, maybe I wouldn't.

14

I felt like a secret agent. I thought about buying some dark glasses and a trench coat, like they wore in the movies.

Trying to keep an eye on Jana was no easy feat. In fact, it was almost impossible. Jana always kept moving. I mean, she never stopped. She was like a hummingbird, flitting from locker to locker or from group to group.

It was also kind of a shock to learn how many actual friends she had. There were trillions of them. They were everywhere. She seemed to know half of Roosevelt already, even though she'd only been going there for a few weeks.

Jana got to school in the morning and headed straight for Main Hall, where they had some bench seats and a huge, ugly statue. Nobody actually sat on the seats, of course. You could stand on them, jump over them, or lean against them. But you definitely could not sit on them.

The really cool kids hung out in Main Hall before school started. It was like a party, without teachers and parents. Of course, there wasn't a whole lot you could do except talk. But it was better than nothing. And *no one* actually wanted to sit in homeroom, just waiting for the bell to ring to start school.

Jana wandered around Main Hall in the morning,

flitting from group to group like she was the hostess at some dinner party. It was weird to watch too. She'd drift over to one group, and the group she'd been talking to would sort of disintegrate a few minutes later. Some of those kids would drift over to where Jana had gone to. Then when Jana left that group, it would soon begin to melt away.

Jana seemed to be the catalyst, the engineer who drove the train. She always seemed to be at the center of every conversation. She was the star, the jewel in the crown.

It was just exactly opposite of the way things were at home. There, she didn't say much during dinner. She was pretty quiet whenever the kids started yelling about things. She mostly kept to herself, when she wasn't talking on the phone.

But not here at school. Here, she was always in the thick of everything. It was like night and day. I couldn't figure it out to save my life. All I knew was that it was the way things were.

This particular morning, I was having a very, very tough time being a secret agent. I couldn't seem to find a place to hang out and keep an eye on Jana. There wasn't anybody in the Main Hall I knew very well. And I couldn't just plant myself in the middle of the place.

What I decided to do, finally, was sit on the stairs that looked out over the hall and pretend to study. Nobody who actually knew me would believe it for a second. But it was all I had.

I'd been there for a few minutes when it happened. It was strange to watch, halfway across the hall. I felt like a fan at a baseball game, almost an observer.

Jana was talking to a small group of girls. They were all standing as close as they possibly could to each other, and talking as fast as they could.

There was a sudden commotion at the other end of the hall, opposite from where I was sitting. Most of the heads turned in that direction. An instant later, Tommy Gun and his entourage entered the hall, clapping loudly for themselves.

It was pretty funny, actually. Tommy Gun was such a clown, really. He and his gang just didn't quite fit into things. Which is why they came in clapping for themselves, I guess. Nobody else was going to pay any attention to them, that was for sure.

They sauntered into the middle of the hall and stopped dead in their tracks. Most of the other kids just stopped talking and stared at them, like you look at the monkeys doing tricks at the zoo, swinging from the bars of their cage.

Tommy Gun stopped clapping for himself. His followers stopped immediately, right on cue. Everybody continued to stare. Nobody twitched a muscle. Tommy Gun and his gang stared back.

Just then, someone moved away from one of the groups and started to walk toward Tommy Gun. Eyes swiveled toward that person, watching her as she approached the gang.

I stared in shock as Jana made her way toward Tommy Gun. I felt so utterly helpless. There was nothing I could do. Absolutely nothing.

Jana stopped just short of the gang and said something to Tommy Gun. I couldn't hear what she said, but there was a smile on her face. There was definitely a smile there.

Tommy Gun said something back to her. The rest of the kids in the hall continued to stare, waiting for some cue.

Tommy Gun reached out and tried to put his arm

around Jana. Jana easily, and shyly, moved away. But she wasn't angry about it. She just moved slightly out of Tommy Gun's reach and continued to talk to him.

The rest of Tommy Gun's gang started to encircle Jana. I almost got up from the stairs and walked over. But I couldn't. I just couldn't. Jana would kill me. She'd *never* forgive me if I did something like that.

No, I was stuck. I'd have to sit where I was and watch this, unable to do or say anything.

Tommy Gun's gang closed in around the two of them, Tommy Gun and Jana. I couldn't see them. The hall was still strangely silent. Everybody seemed to be waiting for something to happen, though I'm sure they didn't know what it was they were waiting for. I know I didn't.

After what seemed like forever, the gang parted and Jana emerged. She had a huge smile on her face, like she'd just done something absolutely wonderful. She drifted back to her knot of friends.

Tommy Gun held up his right arm, his fist raised. "Later!" I heard him call out after Jana.

Jana didn't answer him. But she smiled. Yes, she definitely smiled back at Tommy Gun. There was no mistaking that.

A second later, the hall began to buzz with conversation again. I guess they'd seen what they'd waited to see.

So had I. But I sure didn't like what I'd seen. No, I didn't. Tommy Gun was on the prowl, on the hunt. He was after my sister, and there was absolutely, positively nothing whatsoever I could do about it. Jana would never speak to me if I even tried anything.

15

Karen confirmed my worst fears. Jana was beginning to talk about Tommy Gun, a little. Just a few words here and there. But it was easy to see, Karen said. Jana was fascinated with him. She thought he was interesting, different, funny.

It was starting to drive me crazy. I was so used to just *doing* something when I had to.

If I was losing a tennis match, I just shifted into another gear or tried something else. If I didn't understand something in school, I sought out someone who could explain the problem to me.

But, here, I was totally at a loss. I just didn't know what to do. It was maddening.

"You know, Cally, this really isn't any of our business," Karen told me one night, after she'd given me her report on that day's Tommy Gun sightings.

"Sure it is," I said. "If we don't protect her from that creep, who's going to?"

"But what if she doesn't want to be protected?"

"Then she's crazy," I said angrily. "She just doesn't know the guy, that's all."

"We ought to tell Mom too," Karen said, looking hard at me for help.

I shook my head. I knew it was wrong—or, at least, I was pretty sure it was wrong—but I just couldn't bring myself to rat on Jana. "No, I'm not gonna do that. Jana would never forgive us."

"I know," Karen nodded. "But we should tell Mom, anyway. She'll be mad if she finds out that we knew what was happening and didn't say anything."

"We'll just have to worry about that later," I said.

* * * * *

I woke up that night. But it was too late. The deed had been done. I'm not sure why neither Chris nor I had heard it. We should have heard what was happening. I know I was expecting something like it to happen.

Actually, I do sort of remember hearing something. *Rustle, thud, rustle, thud.* That's what I remember. But it wasn't enough to actually wake me up.

What I saw when I opened my eyes was something white fluttering outside our window. It looked like a ghost. It just fluttered back and forth, back and forth. I must have stared at it for a long time before I finally sat up in bed and really looked at it.

"Chris?" I called out softly.

"Yeah?" he answered.

"You up?"

"No, you moron, I'm still asleep."

I ignored the remark. "Do you see something outside?"

"Yeah. I think we just got hit with toilet paper."

I looked out the window again, at the white ghost fluttering back and forth in front of the window. "Brother!" I muttered. "I thought I heard something like that."

"Then why didn't you get up?"

"I dunno. I just didn't."

"Well, it's too late now."

"I know," I said, slipping down off the top bunk. I walked over to the window. I looked out over the yard. There were streams and streams of toilet paper draped over limbs all throughout our front yard. Boy, did I hope it wouldn't rain later the rest of the night.

"I can't believe this," I grumbled.

"Believe it."

"Why didn't we hear it, Chris?"

"They were quiet this time."

"But how'd they actually manage that? They're always so rowdy."

"I guess they didn't want to get caught."

"Mom's really gonna be steamed."

"Then she's gonna tell us to clean it up," Chris muttered. "Like it's our fault."

I looked out over the yard again. The white streamers of paper just fluttered there in the breeze silently. I sighed. Would this never end?

* * * * *

Jana was thrilled. Absolutely, positively thrilled. No one had ever thrown toilet paper all around her front yard, in her honor, and she was delighted.

"Cool," she said. She was standing in the front yard the next morning, in her pink fluffy slippers.

Mom was standing next to her. She didn't think it was so cool. "Cally, did you hear anything last night?" she asked me.

Chris and I had decided to just wait until morning and let everyone discover it on their own. No need to ruin everyone else's night, we figured. It wasn't like the toilet paper was going anywhere.

"No, Mom," I answered. "At least not while they were doing it. I woke up and thought I heard something, but it was too late."

"And Chris?"

"He didn't hear anything, either."

Chris was smart. He was inside, doing something

else. I guess he figured that if he wasn't outside when Mom discovered the prank, he might not get asked to help clean up the mess. Fat chance.

"Can the two of you clean this up before you go to school?" Mom asked me.

"Chris and me?"

"Yes, Chris and you," Mom said, turning to face me. I think she was expecting an argument about it.

"What about Jana?"

"I don't think this was done by any of her friends," she said, daring me to argue with her. "This looks more like something one of your friends, or one of Chris', would do."

I thought about arguing with her, telling her that I was almost positive Tommy Gun was responsible. But then I'd have to explain about Jana, and I didn't want to get into it.

"But Jana can help if she wants to?" I asked.

"If she wants to."

Mom and I both glanced at Jana. But she wasn't even listening to us. She was staring intently at something.

We both followed Jana's eyes. I don't know why I hadn't noticed it earlier. I guess because it was so crude, it was hard to recognize right away.

There were three large letters hanging from the limbs of a couple of trees. Or, at least, they sure looked like letters. They had to be.

The first letter was an "I." It was just one stream of paper. A few feet to its right was an "L." Someone had tied a second stream—parallel to the ground—from the bottom to a small tree to the right.

The third letter was a "Y." It had clearly been harder to manage. There were two streams of paper coming down. They were tied off in the middle, with one combined stream then hanging down to the ground.

"What does 'ILY' stand for?" Mom asked when she'd figured it out.

"Beats me," I said.

Jana didn't say anything. She was still staring at the three letters with a blank, happy look on her face.

"It stands for 'I Love You,' " Karen said. She must have just joined us. She was still rubbing the sleep out of her eyes.

I glanced back at the letters. "You're right," I said.

"Thank you, I know I am," Karen said.

"But who does this person love?" Mom asked, clearly confused now.

Karen and I looked at each other. What now?

"Ah, who knows?" I shrugged. "It could be somebody's idea of a joke. We'll probably never know."

"But somebody put those letters there for a reason," Mom insisted. "It has to mean something."

"Mom, I don't think we'll ever find out," I said. "No sense racking our brains over it."

Karen was looking at Jana. But Jana was clearly not going to say anything. She wasn't even paying any attention to the conversation. Or, if she was, she sure wasn't letting on about it.

"Yeah, Mom, Cally's probably right," Karen said. "We'll probably never know who did this."

"But it has to mean something," Mom muttered, looking back and forth between Karen and me, probing for the answer to her question. She didn't even look at Jana, for some weird reason.

I shrugged. "Don't know, Mom. Gotta mean something, but I guess we'll never know."

Mom looked me right in the eye. She knew I wasn't telling her the whole truth. She *knew*. I was sure of it. I did my best to look right back at her without wavering, but it wasn't easy. I don't think I succeeded very well.

"All right," Mom sighed at last. "I guess you're both right. We'll probably never find out who did this. And I guess there's no point in telling the police about it. Just a harmless prank."

"Yeah, Chris and I'll have it cleaned up in no time," I said quickly.

"Better get started, then," Mom said, turning back toward the house. "You have about an hour before you need to get to school."

I reached up and tugged on one of the streamers. It came down easily, fluttering to the ground into a heap. "No problem," I grinned. "It might even be fun."

"I'm glad," Mom laughed.

I walked over to Jana, then. "Better get inside, before Mom figures it out," I whispered in her ear.

Jana whirled on me, almost in shock. She looked at me in surprise.

"Do you . . . ?"

"Yeah, I know," I growled. "Better get inside. Quick."

Jana almost said something, but changed her mind at the last instant. She hurried inside without another word. She did glance over her shoulder at me once, though. I jerked my head toward the front door, silently urging her to get inside. She turned and hurried toward the door.

There's an old track out behind the lunchroom at Roosevelt. Once upon a time, it used to be both the school's football field and its track.

But they'd built another field on the other side of the school—a bigger field, with bleachers and everything—and the old track wasn't used now for much of anything except during gym class sometimes.

During lunch, when it was warm outside, you could walk around it. You weren't supposed to step off the track, although kids did it all the time. On the far side, away from the lunchroom, you could drop over a wall and hang out where the lunchroom monitors couldn't see you.

You had to be quick, though. You had to look over your shoulder to see if one of the monitors with the red armband was looking your way, scoot over to the railing that surrounded the track, hop over it, and land about five feet down on the sidewalk. Then you just sort of hung out there until the lunch bell rang.

I never went down there much, because the smokers were starting to take the place over. The place wasn't policed much, so they were starting to hang out there as much as they were the restrooms.

It was one of those days that I really wanted to be somewhere else. Anywhere else but in my fourth period science class.

Because the first frost had come that morning, they'd cranked up the furnaces at Roosevelt. Heat was gushing out of the vents. There was just one problem, though. The frost had given way to a brilliant sun and the day was starting to warm up fast.

That didn't keep the furnace from blasting away, though. Which meant that the rooms were about a billion degrees too hot. I felt like a stuffed turkey roasting in the oven.

All the kids were practically gasping for air, it was so hot. The teachers all said the same thing, that it would cool off as soon as they turned off the furnace. But I think that stupid furnace was on automatic pilot. I kept hearing it turn over "crank-a-crank-a-crank" all morning long.

I was sitting there, gasping for air, staring out the windows that were half covered by steam from the furnace vents, when I spotted Tommy Gun and his gang strolling around the track behind the lunchroom.

I had a perfect view of the track. The science teacher hadn't assigned seats at the start of the year, so I'd been able to snag a seat near one of the windows. That way, I could look out whenever I got bored.

There were three lunch periods at Roosevelt. Karen and I were in the second. Jana was in the first, which was right now. So Tommy Gun was in Jana's lunch period, I thought darkly. Great.

I watched Tommy Gun and his gang stroll around the track. It was sort of interesting to watch from a distance. They'd be walking along, and Tommy Gun would suddenly shove one of his gang sideways, causing him to trip and fall into the grass. The rest of his gang laughed.

Or else Tommy Gun would walk up behind another gang member, twist his arm behind his back until he doubled over. Then Tommy Gun would release him and send him lurching forward. Everybody laughed.

Tommy Gun actually started to jog at one point. Everybody started to jog with him, easily at first. Then Tommy Gun started to race, his arms flailing in all directions. His gang tore after him.

When a few of them started to close the gap, Tommy Gun suddenly thrust his arms high in the air, declaring victory, and then came to a dead stop. They had to stand there for a few moments, gasping for air because all that smoking had cut their endurance.

You had to laugh, watching Tommy Gun parade around outside with his gang. They probably thought the whole world was watching, when really it was only me. Nobody else cared.

While Tommy Gun's gang was doubled over, clutching their sides and trying to catch what little of their breath was left, a second group came into view. It was a smaller group, led by a girl with long, jet-black hair that fell to her waist.

Tommy Gun was the first to spot Jana and her friends, who were doing their level best not to look over their shoulders at the boys. Tommy Gun punched one of his buddies, nearly knocking him over. My blood started to boil. It was all I could do to keep from bolting from the classroom.

Tommy Gun started to shake his head, like he was a rooster about to crow. He was clearly getting himself worked up for the hunt.

For it was, indeed, a hunt. I was sure of that. Positive, in fact. There was no other way to describe the bizarre scene.

Tommy Gun started to stroll after the small group of girls, who promptly started to giggle and bunch close together. Only Jana continued to walk independently, as if she didn't care who was following her.

The rest of Tommy Gun's gang struggled to catch up to their leader. They all started to stroll casually. The girls, except Jana, giggled and bunched even closer.

Tommy Gun's gang started to close in on the girls. Jana never looked over her shoulder. She just kept marching around the track, like she was in a race or something.

They meandered around the track like that—Tommy Gun and his gang shadowing the girls—for a couple of laps. It was really strange to watch.

On the third time around—when they were on the far side of the track, near the railing that dropped over the side—Tommy Gun must have said something. The girls all stopped, even Jana, and turned around to face the gang. There were only a few feet separating them.

Jana started to walk back toward Tommy Gun. I was gripping the side of my desk so hard I was starting to bend the hard plastic.

Jana got right up in Tommy Gun's face. She flipped her hair back over her shoulder, catching Tommy Gun in the face. She said something. He answered. Jana said something else. Tommy Gun answered.

Jana looked over at her friends. She turned back to Tommy Gun and said something. Tommy Gun glanced at his pals, and jerked his head over his shoulder toward the railing.

Jana huddled with her friends. Tommy Gun huddled with his. I spotted a couple of low-fives.

The huddles broke. A decision had been reached. The girls drifted toward Tommy Gun's gang and, with a quick glance over their shoulders to see if there were any lunchroom monitors watching, bolted toward the railing.

Most of Tommy Gun's gang ran for the railing and got to the other side as quickly as they could. So did most of the girls. Only Jana and Tommy Gun walked, slowly, toward the railing.

Tommy Gun tried to put an arm around Jana's shoulder. Jana brushed it aside. Tommy Gun tried again. Jana pushed it away, more forcefully this time. She said something to Tommy Gun, who just shrugged and kept walking.

When they got to the railing, Jana didn't even look over her shoulder. She just climbed over the railing quickly and jumped to the ground a few feet below, disappearing from my view. Tommy Gun disappeared an instant later.

I slammed my fist down on the side of my desk so hard it rattled my books. One of them dropped to the floor, making a *whap* sound when it hit. Everyone turned to look at me.

"Is everything all right, Mr. James?" the science teacher asked.

"Yeah, um, sure," I mumbled. "Sorry about that."

"Are you quite sure everything's all right?"

"Yeah, everything's fine," I said sheepishly. "I just knocked my books over."

"Good," the teacher nodded. "Then perhaps you can answer the question before the class."

"Sure," I said confidently. I paused. The class tittered. "Maybe you could repeat the question?"

The teacher sighed and glared at me. I just barely managed to keep from glancing out the window again. He repeated the question. I answered it dutifully, thankful that it was something I'd actually studied the night before.

As the class returned to normal, I just sat in my chair dully, wondering what I could possibly do.

Probably nothing. If I tried to do something, it would just send Jana hurtling toward Tommy Gun. I was sure of that. I knew Jana. If I jumped in, not only would she be furious, she'd do exactly opposite of what I wanted her to.

But I couldn't just ignore what was happening. I had to do *something*. I just had to. There was no way I was going to let that jerk mess around with Jana. No way.

I couldn't tell Mom, though. That wouldn't work. I could tell Karen, but that probably wouldn't have any effect. I could confront Tommy Gun, but he'd only laugh in my face.

So what could I do? Sit here in this blast furnace of a room and sweat, that's what. And wonder just what in the world Jana and Tommy Gun were doing together on the other side of that railing.

I redoubled my efforts to spy on Jana. It was hard. Actually, it was almost impossible. Jana always gave me strange looks if she saw me just hanging around. So I had to figure out ways to keep an eye on her without letting on that I was actually spying on her.

Karen wasn't much help in this effort, either. Jana wasn't talking at all these days, which meant that Karen would have to pry to get anything out of Jana.

After three days of driving myself crazy, I decided I just had to know what Jana was up to. I'd sat in my science room three days in a row and watched Jana and Tommy Gun go through this routine. It was absolutely maddening watching it.

Every day it was almost the same thing. Tommy Gun's gang would parade around the track like peacocks, and then Jana's "gang" would come out of the lunchroom and follow them a little later. Soon after, they'd all disappear over the railing.

On the fourth day, I really did a rotten thing. I knew it was wrong, but I didn't know what else to do. Karen helped me, even though she knew it was wrong too. We forged Mom's signature on a piece of paper that said I had a doctor's appointment during my fourth period class the next day.

"Cally, you know this is wrong," Karen told me. We

were up in the loft. Chris was downstairs watching TV.

"I know it," I snapped. "But what choice do I have? It's the only way I can see what's going on."

"But it's still wrong," Karen insisted. "You, of all people, should know that."

"What's that supposed to mean?"

"You know."

"No, I don't," I said impatiently. "Tell me."

"You're a Christian, or at least you always tell me that you are," she said hesitantly. "And now you're, like, deliberately doing something that you know is wrong . . . "

I glared at Karen. She was right, of course. There was no squirming out of this one. But I had to do something. And this was so harmless. No one would get hurt.

"But what am I supposed to do?" I pleaded with her. "What can I do? This is all I've been able to think of."

"But it's wrong, isn't it?"

"Yeah, I guess it's wrong," I admitted. "Sort of."

"Then you shouldn't do it," Karen said firmly. "I just don't think you should. That's all."

"Look, will you write the note or not?"

"If you tell me to, I will," Karen said softly, gazing at me intently. "But it's still wrong."

I looked away uneasily. I knew, in my heart, that Karen was right. Absolutely, perfectly right. What I was doing was wrong. I was deceiving Mom, the school, my teachers. But it was for a noble cause. This was the only way I could find out, for sure, what Jana was up to.

God, I thought, *I know You'll put this one down as a big mistake in that book of Yours. I know that. But I'm*

*willing to risk it. I have to look out for Jana. If I don't,
no one else will. And I just don't see any other way. I
really don't.*

Part of me knew that I wasn't really listening to God
for help. I wasn't paying real close attention. If I
asked, there would be a way. There always is. God
helps you find those ways through the really hard
parts.

But I didn't see one here—a way through the hard
part, I mean—so I figured I had to do something. And
what I planned to do really wasn't all that evil or
anything. God would surely forgive me. My intentions
were honorable.

The plan was simple. I'd turn the note into the principal's office first thing in the morning, then slip outside after my third period class and position myself
across the street from the track and watch from the
bushes to see what Jana was up to. Simple as that.

In reality, it was pretty crummy. Spying on your
sister, I mean. But I'd thought about it endlessly, and I
didn't see any other choice. There was just no other
way to find out, for sure, what Jana and Tommy Gun
were doing. And I couldn't just confront them.

That's probably another one, God, I thought miser-
ably. *You can put that one down in Your book too,
right next to the part about forging Mom's signature.*

A good thing Jesus said that once He's entered your
heart, all things will be forgiven. I need it. Boy, do I.
Seems like I'm always messing up, sometimes
intentionally.

"You have to sign the note," I told Karen with determination. "There's no other way."

Karen looked at me for a second, just to make sure I
was serious, then she set to her task. She took out a
nice piece of Mom's personal stationery she'd brought

with her—that would be a nice touch—and then wrote in careful script: "Please excuse Cally during his fourth period, as he has a doctor's appointment. Sincerely, Marilynn James."

I glanced over Karen's shoulder. "Wow," I muttered. "That's pretty good. It looks just like Mom's signature."

"Thanks," Karen said proudly. "I doodle sometimes during class, when I'm bored."

I took the note from Karen, folded it once, carefully, and tucked it in my books for school the next day. I was already starting to sweat, just thinking about the scam.

"I'll let you know what I find out," I said.

"I think I already know," Karen said glumly.

"You do?"

"Sure. For one thing, she always carries these breath mints around in her purse now. She never did before."

"What's that mean?" I asked, a little confused.

"To cover up the smell, on her breath," Karen scowled. "Don't you know anything?"

"The smell?"

"From the cigarettes. I'm sure she's trying to smoke, so she bought the mints to cover up."

"Man, is that ever stupid."

"Jana probably thinks it's cool," Karen said grimly. "She goes for stuff like that."

"You're pretty sure about this?"

"Not positive," Karen answered. "But I'm pretty sure. I know Jana."

"Well," I sighed. "We'll definitely know after tomorrow."

"I guess so," Karen said, her lips pursed in thought. "I just can't believe that Jana's actually doing this,"

I said, shaking my head. "It doesn't make any sense."

"Jana does things her own way."

"Even when they're dumb?"

"Especially then," Karen laughed. "She likes to try things. Even dumb things."

I glanced over at the note that was now tucked in my books. I guess I like to try things too. But I'm not quite as willing to go out as far on the limb.

But was there any difference, really, between what I was doing and what Jana was doing?

Sure, it was wrong for Jana to smoke and to date Tommy Gun behind Mom's back—if, in fact, that's what she was doing—but it was also just as wrong for me to get Mom's signature forged and to not tell my mom what was going on.

Where did you draw the line?

----●18

I skipped most of breakfast the next morning. I wanted to get to school early and scout things out a little bit, so I just grabbed a doughnut and gulped down a glass of orange juice before hurrying out the door.

Mom almost stopped me. She hated it when we didn't eat a proper breakfast. It drove her crazy. But, fortunately, she just let me off this morning with a stern glare and a warning that I shouldn't expect to get by with only a doughnut for breakfast in the future.

"Sure, Mom," I said quickly, jamming the rest of the doughnut in my mouth. I made sure my backpack was zipped—the faked note still carefully tucked inside one of my books—and slung it over my back.

"I mean it, Cally," Mom said firmly. "You set an example for the rest of the kids. If you don't eat right in the morning, they won't either."

"Mom, nobody else is here yet," I said, glancing around the kitchen just to make sure.

"You know what I mean, young man," Mom said.

"Okay, okay, I gotcha," I answered quickly. "But it's just that I want to get to school early today."

"Why is today so special?" Mom asked easily, turning back to the stove, where she was fixing eggs and cheese.

Oops. *I really walked into that one,* I thought. "Oh, nothin', really," I answered as nonchalantly as I could. "There's just somethin' I gotta do."

"What?"

Boy, if I don't do something quickly, I'll be forced to lie to Mom, I thought in a panic. *Then there'll be a third entry in God's book, right next to the forged note and the part about not telling Mom.*

"Just school stuff," I said, moving toward the door. "Mom, I really have to go." I opened the door and started to leave.

"Cally!" Mom said sternly.

I stopped in the doorway, holding my breath. I was sure she was going to demand to know where I was going, what I was about to do. And I'd be forced to lie through my teeth.

"Be careful," she said, instead. "It's darker out there this early in the morning. The cars might not see you as easily."

"I'll be careful," I said, nodding fervently. "I promise."

"Good," she said, turning back to the stove.

I slammed the door and breathed a huge sigh of relief. *That* had certainly been close. I couldn't help wondering, though, if getting prepared to lie through your teeth was the same as actually lying. That probably went in the book too, I thought glumly. Oh well.

I zipped up my windbreaker before climbing on my bike. It was starting to get chilly, now that it was getting toward the end of September. It reminded me that I'd need to remember to get something warm to wear for warm-ups for our first tennis match later in the week.

Just as I'd predicted, the coach had made Evan Grant and me cocaptains. We were going to alternate at the number one spot on the team, and play doubles together. He'd never even made us play each other to see who would be number one. That was just as well, I figured.

It was going to be interesting, playing doubles with Evan. We'd have to get used to each other. Our styles were so different. But that, perhaps, was why we'd make excellent doubles partners.

I mapped out my plan as I rode to school. Mom had been right. It was pretty dark outside now. I stayed well off the road when there weren't any sidewalks, just to make doubly sure.

My plan was to park my bike, drop my books off at my locker, and then wander around the track and the railing to see if I could find a good spot from which to spy on Jana and Tommy Gun. I might not have a chance to do it later in the day, when there might be more people around, like a gym class out on the field or something.

There was almost no one at the school when I arrived. I don't think I'd ever gotten there quite so early. The halls were practically empty.

I spotted Evan Grant walking down another hall I was approaching. I almost called out to him, but he was already gone by the time I got to the corridor. I only caught a glimpse of him as he disappeared down another corridor when I'd turned the corner.

Now, where is he going? I wondered. *I didn't know Evan got to school so early. What can he possibly be doing here at this time of day?*

I decided I had enough time to follow him, just to see. I was curious, so I hurried down the hall to find him.

When I turned the corner, I spotted him as he disappeared into the gym. I hustled down that way and stood outside the double doors at the far corner of the gym, staring in.

Evan was shucking some warm-ups under one of the backboards on the basketball court. He had gym shorts and a shirt underneath. He tossed his warm-ups against the wall, on top of a big duffel bag that he'd brought with him. *His school clothes must be in there,* I figured.

Evan started to jog across the basketball court. I stood there, transfixed, and just watched as he jogged back and forth across the court. On the next trip down the court, he picked up the pace. He picked it up yet again on the next trip. By the fourth time down the court, he was into a full sprint.

I couldn't believe it. I just couldn't. Evan Grant, who almost oozed self-confidence and an air that he *never* practiced much, was here at school early, doing wind sprints in the gym!

So that explained why he didn't tire out in his practice matches with me. I'd always sort of wondered about that, in the back of my mind.

I opened the door quietly and started to meander into the gym. Evan spotted me in the middle of a sprint, as I was coming into the gym. He didn't slow down, but sprinted all the way to the end.

"So that's how you do it," I called out to him as I kept walking.

"Do what?" Evan huffed. He was doubled over, clutching the bottom of his shorts, practically pulling them down to his knees.

"Keep up your wind during matches."

"How'd you think I did it, you ignoramus?" Evan said sarcastically. "Magic or something?"

"I dunno," I shrugged as I reached his side. "I just sort of figured it came naturally."

Evan snorted, still puffing. "You don't get in shape by sitting around eating ice cream cones. I don't think it exactly works that way."

"I know that!" I said. "I just meant that I figured you got in shape with the tennis practice."

"Maybe *you* do, the way you charge around the court like some loco bull in a china shop—"

"I don't play like that," I said darkly.

"You know what I mean," Evan sighed. "I don't have that luxury because I sit at the baseline, hardly moving around. If I don't do something like this, I won't be in shape."

"Well, I never figured—"

"Yeah, I know," Evan grinned. "And I wasn't about to let you in on it, either. I wanted to keep you guessing."

I laughed. "That's a great way for a partner to act."

Evan looked up at me. "That's right, I forgot. We're partners now, aren't we?"

"You bet. First match is this week."

"I know," Evan grimaced. "How're we ever going to manage to actually play together as a team?"

"Ah, we'll manage somehow."

"Maybe. And if we do, I was thinking . . . "

I looked at Evan, wondering what was on his mind. "Yeah?"

"Well, you know, this year we both go into the 14s at the national championships. We'll be going up against kids a year older than us. Which means that we both might get bumped off early."

"I know," I nodded. "I've been thinking about it too. But it'll be a good learning experience. I didn't figure to do anything there this year."

Evan looked at me. "But we could win the championship, I think, as a doubles team. With your serve, and my baseline game, we could do it," he said firmly.

"Maybe. It's something to think about."

"Yeah, think about it," Evan said quickly, standing again. He stepped to the line, ready to start another wind sprint.

"I will. I promise."

"Okay. Well, see ya. Okay?"

"Okay."

Evan sprinted away. It was amazing to me to think how, not so long ago, he and I had been archenemies. We still were, but in a different way now. We were friendly rivals, both on and off the court. It would be strange playing with him as part of a team.

I glanced at my watch. I'd lost some time talking to Evan. Some of the kids would be starting to arrive at school now. The bus that Jana came in on had probably arrived by now, I figured.

I hurried out of the gym and to my locker, dropped my books off, and headed toward the lunchroom. The place was curiously alive with bustling cooks when I arrived. There was rock music echoing in the empty lunchroom as I walked through.

I guess it had never really occurred to me that it might take the kitchen cooks the entire morning to prepare lunch for hundreds of kids. I'd always sort of assumed that the lunches had just arrived there somehow.

The sun was starting to come up as I went out the back, toward the old track. It was peeking over the rooftops of the houses nearby, casting long shadows across the old field.

I walked straight across the field, toward the railing. I scuffed my tennis shoes through the frost on the field, throwing flecks onto my pants, where they quickly melted.

I wasn't really paying a whole lot of attention to anything, so I never even had a chance. I just stumbled right into it.

I walked up to the railing, put one hand on it and hopped over. It was about a five-foot drop to the other side, and tingles shot up both legs as I hit the ground.

I landed just a few feet away from Jana and Tommy Gun. I turned, and there they were. We all looked at each other in almost near-total shock. None of us said anything right away. We were all too stunned.

Jana had her back to the wall. A half-burned cigarette butt dangled from her mouth. The lighted end of the cigarette seemed to shoot into my mind like an orange laser. I'd never seen anything so ugly.

Tommy Gun was facing her, one arm propped up against the wall, sort of crooked behind Jana's neck. An almost-finished cigarette butt dangled from his mouth as well. Both of Jana's arms were wrapped around Tommy Gun's waist. Tommy Gun's other hand rested on her shoulder.

I blinked once, twice. Tommy Gun and Jana didn't budge from their casual, near-embrace. They seemed to be locked together, in a tangled pose.

Tommy Gun finally broke the spell. He took his hand off Jana's shoulder, took a long pull on his cigarette, and then flicked it off to the side, into the street.

"Well, if it ain't the big brother, lookin' out for little sis," Tommy Gun sneered.

I didn't answer. I couldn't help it. I was still staring at Jana, in shock. I guess I'd just never imagined that this was, in fact, even possible. But it had to be. Here it was, in all its glory.

Jana pulled the cigarette butt from her mouth without taking another drag. She moved it behind her back and let it drop to the ground.

"What're you doin' here, Cally?" she asked.

I could see the pain, and the anger, in her eyes. "Don't worry, Jana," I said quickly. "I won't tell Mom."

"You'd *better* not," she said, her dark eyes flashing.

"Can you trust him?" Tommy Gun asked Jana.

I clenched my fists. Jana must have seen it out of the corner of her eye, because she pulled Tommy Gun a little closer to her. It almost made me sick to my stomach.

"Of course I can trust him," she said softly. "He's my brother."

"So?" Tommy Gun growled. "He ratted on me. He might do the same with you."

"He won't," Jana said confidently, glancing at me to make sure.

"Look, I said I wouldn't, and I won't," I said, my hands still clenched at my sides.

"I wouldn't be so sure," Tommy Gun said, giving me a sly wink that Jana couldn't see. "He's been a creep about things. I know *I* don't trust him."

I took a step toward Tommy Gun. It took every single, solitary ounce of willpower I possessed to keep from taking those remaining steps that separated the three of us.

"Jana knows she can trust me," I managed to say. It was getting harder to talk. My throat was starting to get very, very dry.

"Yeah, well, maybe she *doesn't* know that," Tommy Gun said before my sister could answer.

"Look, you—" I started to say.

Jana cut me off, quickly untangling herself and stepping in between Tommy Gun and me. Her face was flushed, but there was no mistaking the determination in her eyes.

"Cally, please," she pleaded. "Just leave."

I stared at her, not quite sure what to do or say. I decided I couldn't just let it go by anymore. I *had* to say something. "You're a complete dope to smoke," I said to her. "You know that, don't you?"

"It's my choice, not yours," she fired back.

"Mom would lose it if she knew about you and this . . . this jerk," I said, looking at Tommy Gun.

"You're the real jerk!" Tommy Gun yelled.

Jana leaned against Tommy Gun, keeping him from moving toward me. "Mom isn't gonna find out, is she?" Jana said.

"Not from me, she isn't," I said. "You oughta tell her yourself."

"Maybe I will," Jana said evasively. "Either way, it's none of your business what I do. So just leave, would ya?"

I looked at Jana, then at Tommy Gun, then back at Jana.

"All right, I'm leavin'," I muttered in defeat.

"Thanks, Cally," my sister said softly.

"Beat it, sucker," Tommy Gun taunted for good measure.

I took one more step toward the two of them. "I'm leaving because my sister asked me to, not because of you," I said, looking directly at Tommy Gun.

"Yeah, sure," he growled.

"And don't worry, we'll see each other again," I vowed to him.

"Oooohh, I'm worried," said Tommy Gun.

I didn't answer. I looked at Jana again, shook my head sadly, then turned and left. I heard Tommy Gun pull his pack of cigarettes from his pocket and pop it twice to get a new one out as I walked away. It almost sounded like gunfire.

19

I was still in a state of shock as I walked back into the school. I just could not believe what I'd actually witnessed. What a coincidence. I simply could not believe that I'd stumbled into the two of them like that.

Then I remembered the forged note in my backpack. I almost started laughing. I guess there was no need for that, not now. No need to deceive the school, or forge Mom's signature, or skip school and spy on Jana.

A sudden, cold chill swept through me. How strange. In a way I had certainly not expected, God had opened a door for me that allowed me to confront Jana without deception or lies.

I was sure He was responsible. The timing had been perfect, too perfect. I'd seen Evan Grant in the hallway, which kept me just long enough so that I could stumble into Jana and Tommy Gun as they were hanging out together before school started.

So, without any chance to prepare for it, Jana and I had been thrown together. It was all out in the open, where it ought to be. There was no deception any longer, on either Jana's part or mine.

Amazing, I thought, *truly amazing.* I opened my backpack, took out the forged note, and crumpled it up without looking at it again. Karen would be relieved to know that I'd never actually used it.

I tossed it into a trash can as I walked back into the school. *Good riddance,* I thought. *And thank You, God, for opening that door and letting me off the hook.*

* * * * *

Boy, now I'd done it, though. Not only was I responsible for sending Tommy Gun chasing after my sister, I'd pretty much pledged not to tell Mom or do anything about it.

No, that wasn't exactly true. I could do something about it. I just had no idea what it might be.

I think I sleepwalked through my first three classes. I don't think I heard a single thing any of my teachers said. It was a good thing none of them ever asked me any questions. I'd have given them a blank stare for an answer.

I just kept turning the situation over and over in my mind. I knew I had to do something. I was responsible. I was. There was no turning away from that, as much as I wanted to. So I had to do something.

I cringed as I walked into my fourth period science class. I'd have to sit and look out the window at the hunt again, at the ridiculous game that would be played out on the old field yet again.

I actually tried to sit there and keep from looking out the window. But I couldn't keep myself from stealing glances out the window.

Tommy Gun and his gang showed up, right on cue. A few minutes later, the group of girls who hung out with Jana during lunch also showed up. But Jana wasn't with them. I waited and waited for her to make an appearance, but she never did.

Now, that sure was strange. I wondered what had happened. Where was Jana? Why hadn't she come outside to see Tommy Gun?

* * * * *

"Maybe she's changed her mind and dropped Tommy Gun," Karen offered at lunch.

"No way," I said. "If you'd seen the two of them, like I did, you'd know that wasn't possible."

I'd just finished telling Karen what had happened. As I'd predicted, she'd been relieved that I had never actually had to use the forged note to skip my fourth period class.

"But something happened," Karen said.

I shrugged. "She's probably just thinkin' about things. I would, if I were Jana."

Karen pursed her lips. She was clearly thinking about something. "You know," she said slowly, "it's probably something else."

"What?"

"Jana's probably thinking that she'll have to go underground, now."

"Underground?"

"Yeah, you know, see Tommy Gun in secret. Stuff like that. She won't be able to be so open about it."

"Like seeing Tommy Gun on the old field during lunch." I nodded. It made sense.

"Or smoking out there where you saw the two of them," Karen added.

"You know, I think you're right," I said.

"Which means it will be almost impossible now to ever catch the two of them at anything."

I wrinkled up my nose. "I don't think I'd want to, even if I had the chance."

Karen shook her head. "I can't believe Jana's making such a big mistake. Tommy Gun's such a . . . creepy guy."

"Everybody makes mistakes," I said, gazing intently at Karen.

"I know."

"I mean, I think I remember someone getting in a car and going down to Alabama, when maybe she shouldn't have," I said softly.

Karen looked up sharply. "Don't remind me, okay?" she said, the pain clearly evident in her voice. "I know I made a mistake. Now."

"Sometimes it's hard to see," I said.

"I guess we'll just have to show Jana, somehow."

"I'm not sure it'll do any good with Jana."

"Maybe not, but we have to try, don't we?" Karen asked. "You never gave up with me, so we shouldn't give up with Jana."

20

I don't know why I went by the boys restroom near the gym after school. I just did. There was a still, small voice somewhere in the back of my mind that seemed to guide me toward it. The restroom was on the way to the locker room, anyway. So it was no big deal to drop by it.

I wasn't sure what I'd do when I got there, though. Did I want to face Tommy Gun again? Did I want to pick a fight with him? Did I just want to say something to him again? And if so, what?

I didn't really have a plan. Not really. There was some vague idea about punching him in the nose and maybe sending him to the hospital. But I couldn't do that, if for no other reason than it would mean I'd be kicked off the tennis team again. And I wasn't going to let that happen.

So why was I stepping into Tommy Gun's territory again? I don't really know. I just knew I had to. There was something there, something I wasn't paying attention to.

My hands were ice-cold as I pushed the door open that led into the restroom. I didn't hesitate, though. I marched right in.

The place was empty. There was a horrible, stale smell in the air, a nasty kind of smell that seemed to seep right through my clothes. I knew I'd have to put my clothes right in the wash when I got home.

There were cigarette butts everywhere—in the sink, on the floor, in the trash. What a job the janitor had with this place every night, I thought. *What a crummy, rotten job he must have.* I felt sorry for him.

I looked at my reflection in the mirror. I couldn't see myself very well because of the film over it. Boy, was this place vile. How could anyone in their right mind actually spend any time in here?

I pushed open one of the stalls, just to see what was in there. More cigarette butts mostly. There must have been thirty of them in the toilet. I flushed it and watched with some satisfaction as the water carried them down to some unknown destination.

The stall door swung closed behind me. I turned and started to open it, but then stopped dead in my tracks. In big, bold strokes, for all the world to see — or, at least, for those who passed through this awful place—someone had written something on the bathroom stall door.

"For a *real* good time, call Jana James," it read in big, black Magic Marker. Then it gave Jana's private telephone number, the one she gave out only to her friends. Until now, at least. Now, the whole world could have her number. And they could call her for a real good time. Just great.

I stood there, staring at the door, for the longest time. Finally, still in a kind of trance, I moved past the door, grabbed a handful of paper towels, ran some water over them, and went back in.

I rubbed as hard as I could, but the black Magic Marker had hardened. I didn't even make a dent. Whoever had written this had made his mark for good. Jana James' private telephone number would be up here for a while.

I could feel something beginning to snap inside me. I could feel it coming, and I didn't know what to do about it.

This was over the line. This was no longer a game, as far as I was concerned. Everything had gotten just a little out of hand, and it was time I did something about it. Jana's honor was at stake. And, whether Jana liked it or not, I was going to defend that honor.

21

I didn't have a plan, of course. So what else was new? Tommy Gun was out there, somewhere, and I would find him eventually. That's as far as my planning went.

Dinnertime was really, really hard that night, though. When she wasn't glaring at me through angry, sullen eyes, Jana just picked at her food. I couldn't tell if any food actually made it to her mouth.

I couldn't bring myself to tell Jana about the message in the boys restroom. The way I figured it, Jana wouldn't blame Tommy Gun for it, and it would just hurt her to know that such a message was scrawled out there in such a terrible place.

So I kept it to myself. I was keeping a lot to myself these days, more than I ought to. My struggles with silence were growing longer and more complicated by the minute, it seemed.

It was a good thing God was there to listen to my bumbling attempts to do the right thing, though. A very good thing. It was what kept me going in the right direction.

Jana went straight to her room after dinner. She was on the telephone for the rest of the evening. Beats me who she was talking to. Karen hardly ever went in the room while Jana was on the phone, and Jana certainly wasn't talking about it.

I must have looked over at Mom a hundred times that night, wondering if maybe I shouldn't tell her what I was wrestling with. I wanted to talk to her about it. I really did. She'd know just what to do. I was sure of that.

But I couldn't take that first step. It seemed like such a betrayal of Jana, and I didn't want to push her any further away from me than she was already.

So I sat there, stone-faced, barely paying attention to the TV shows that flickered across the screen. Every so often I could hear Jana's muffled voice drift down the stairs, and I cringed.

"Cally, are you all right?" Mom asked me at one point. She was reading in the recliner across the room, where she could keep an eye on everyone.

"Sure, Mom," I said, startled.

"Positive? You seem worried about something."

"No, it's nothing," I said quickly. "I'm fine. Really."

"You're not worried about your first tennis match this week, are you?"

"I, um, I guess I'm thinking about it a little," I said, glad for the distraction. "I don't want to let the team down."

"Don't worry, you won't."

"The team we're playing finished second in their sectional last year. Their number one is 14, and he's pretty good."

Mom smiled. "I'm sure you'll do fine, Cally. You always do."

"I hope so," I said grimly.

"So is that it, is that what's bothering you?"

I looked down at my shoes. I was squirming now. No question about it. If I didn't move fast and do something, I was going to be in big trouble.

"It's just different things, Mom," I said finally.

"Nothing really important, I guess. I'll figure it out eventually."

Mom didn't answer. She looked at me across the room. She knew there was more to this. She could read me like a book. She'd always been able to practically read my mind, and I was sure my thoughts were beaming away like a neon sign right now.

But she didn't press me. I was thankful for that. Because I wouldn't have been able to resist her. I'd have spilled my guts, and I thought Jana would hate me forever.

"Just tell me about it when you're ready, Cally. Okay? Promise?"

"I promise," I answered, breathing a huge, inward sigh of relief. I turned back to face the television, and Mom turned back to her book.

But I knew she was still glancing my way every so often. As always, she kept a careful, watchful eye on me, even as she let me stumble along my own path.

I heard the seventh stair creak. The seventh stair makes a very distinct noise when someone steps on it. That's how I knew that whoever was sneaking out in the middle of the night was almost to the bottom of the stairs.

I completely woke up almost instantly. I grabbed my watch from the desk, my jeans from the floor, a shirt from the dirty laundry, shoes from under the bed, and got dressed swiftly in the darkness. I was careful not to wake Chris.

It was possible that Jana was going downstairs to get some juice or something. But I didn't think so. Something was going on. Every part of me could feel it.

I made my way down the stairs quickly, careful to avoid the seventh stair.

I heard some movement out on the front porch. I ducked into the shadows beside the steps that led into the living room. An instant later, I heard some rustling. Jana hustled across the living room, opened the front door quietly, and then vanished into the night.

I had to move fast now, or I'd lose her. I glided across the floor, peered out the front door and then, when I was sure it was clear, opened it as well and slipped outside.

Jana was rustling around in the garage. She was probably looking for her bike—an ugly, pink thing that barely moved. She'd have a tough time keeping up in that thing. I ducked into the bushes to wait.

She emerged with a bike, all right—Chris' nice BMX. Boy, if Chris knew Jana was taking that thing out on the road, chewing up the tires, he'd have a cow.

I waited until Jana was walking the bike down the driveway before I ducked into the garage as well and grabbed my own bike. I hustled it out of the garage as quietly as I could.

I could hear Jana still walking her bike with someone. I could hear their muffled, whispered voices.

"Come on, we gotta hurry or we'll miss it," I heard someone call out in a loud stage whisper from the front of our driveway.

"Cool your jets, dude," answered Tommy Gun. "We're comin'."

Miss it? I wondered. *What were they doing? And why was Jana going with them? Was this her indoctrination? Was she becoming part of the "gang" tonight?*

"We got five minutes to get to the Quick Shop if we're gonna make it in time to catch the truck," I heard Squirrel say.

"I said we're comin'!" Tommy Gun hissed.

I was pretty sure I knew which Quick Shop they were talking about. It wasn't more than a few minutes away. I knew a shortcut to it that I was sure these guys didn't know. I'd just have to avoid a couple of dogs on chains two streets away.

I turned around and headed toward the back of our house. I let the bike glide down the hill in our backyard. It would be tough in the dark, but my eyes were already starting to adjust.

There were goose pimples on my arms. Like a

numbskull, I'd forgotten to grab my windbreaker, and my arms were freezing from the chilly night air. It was really starting to become fall.

A dog started to bark at me two houses down. I knew it wouldn't come after me, but I still stepped up the pace just in case. I tore between two houses, jumped the curb, and kept pedaling until I was well down the street.

Three turns later, and I was there. The "Quick Shop" sign was burning brightly in the night. The place was open 24 hours a day.

There was just one car in the parking lot in front of the store. I glanced at my watch as I eased my bike over to one side of the store, deep in the shadows, and waited. It was about two in the morning.

Tommy Gun's gang arrived a couple of minutes later. They too were careful to stay on the fringes of the light cast by the lone street light in front of the store. They pushed their bikes off into the weeds near the road and disappeared from view. They were clearly waiting for something.

A truck rumbled into view—a big, lumbering one, the kind that makes deliveries to stores like this. It was a "Hostess" truck, full of all kinds of cakes and pies and other goodies. The truck creaked to a stop, and a young guy walked around the back, pulled the back end up, and started to unload boxes onto his dolly.

Tommy Gun and his gang made their move about a minute after the guy had entered the store. I watched in disbelief as they ran across the parking lot toward the truck—making sure the truck was in between them and the store—and entered the open door at the back.

Jana was with them. I could definitely see her long,

black hair trailing behind her as she sprinted across the parking lot with the gang. There was no mistaking that.

They didn't make much noise as they raided the truck, stuffing cakes and pies in pockets. Someone had brought a bag. I could hear the *plop, plop* as the goodies were tossed into it.

I was so angry, I could barely even see straight. I wondered vaguely if Jana even knew what she was doing. Did she know she could go to juvenile detention hall for this? This was an actual, real crime. They sent grown-ups to jail for this kind of thing.

But I'm sure Jana figured she'd never get caught. The worst that could happen was that the guy who drove the truck would come back and grab one of them. And that one kid would never squeal.

They all made it out well before the delivery guy returned. They were back to their bikes—with their booty firmly in hand—long before he emerged from the store.

Now where? I thought. The gang was already vanishing from the scene of the crime. I eased my bike out of the shadows and climbed aboard. I was just starting to pedal into the parking lot.

"Hey, you! Hey, kid!" the delivery guy yelled at me.

I turned and looked over my shoulder at him. No way was I stopping to talk to this guy. He'd probably think I had something to do with what had just happened. I started to pedal away.

The guy saw me take off and dropped his dolly. He started to sprint after me. A shock of fear shuddered through my body even as I pushed against the pedals as hard as I could. I didn't look over my shoulder as I hit the street pavement, but I could hear the guy gaining ground.

I pedaled madly, and gradually I heard the *clomp, clomp* of his boots start to fade. Finally, they stopped. "I'm calling the cops on ya, kid!" he called out.

Great, I thought. *Just great.* I could just imagine explaining this to Mom when the cops showed up at my door. But the guy didn't know who I was. He'd never seen me before, and he'd only glanced at me as I tore away.

I eased back into my seat, letting the bike coast. My whole body was shaking from the fear that had rocked me. It was a rotten feeling.

Now, where did those guys go? They had to go somewhere where they could enjoy their ill-gotten gains.

There was a kiddie park nearby, where Mom sometimes took Timmy and Susan. There were swings and a pretty neat fort. They could hang out there while they munched away. I turned right down the next street and headed in that direction.

Sure enough, I heard their voices as I drew near. I slowed and approached the park cautiously. I walked the bike the last 100 feet or so, keeping to the shadows off to the side of the road that led to the park.

They were all hanging out in and around the fort. They were still giving each other high-fives, delighted with the success of their mission. I didn't hear any female voices—other than Jana's—so I figured she must have been the only girl along.

I got as close as I dared and settled down to wait for their next move. I wasn't sure what I was doing out there. Actually, I felt kind of stupid. It didn't make any sense. Something was driving me, though, and I just kept going, not thinking about it.

"Jana, you were an ace," I heard Tommy Gun say. "A real pro."

"Yeah, you were great," Squirrel added.

"It was easy," Jana said breathlessly. I could hear the excitement in her voice. I could tell she'd gotten a charge out of it.

"It isn't always that easy," Tommy Gun warned. "Sometimes, the delivery guys see us and chase after us. You gotta be quick, then, to get away."

"I could do it," Jana said confidently.

I thought about that guy who'd just chased after me and shuddered. I wondered if, in fact, Jana could have so easily outdistanced him.

"The next one won't be so easy," Squirrel said.

"Um, what next one?" Jana asked uneasily.

"You didn't think we'd just hit that place, did ya?" Squirrel cackled. "That was a piece o' cake." I heard Squirrel whack somebody on the back. "Hey, that's funny. Piece o' cake. Get it?"

"Yeah, I get it," Tommy Gun answered. I heard a *thud.*

"Ouch, that hurt!" Squirrel yelled. "Why'd you slug me?"

"Just because," Tommy Gun said viciously.

I could see Jana moving around, near the fort. It didn't look like she was eating any of the cakes and stuff they'd brought back. "What's next?" she asked again.

I could almost see Tommy Gun smile broadly. "A house. We been watchin' it for a coupla' days now."

"A house?" Jana asked, clearly confused. "What do you do with a house?"

"You go in it, ya Ding-Dong," Squirrel said. "Get it? Ding-Dong?"

"Yeah, I get it," Tommy Gun said, slugging Squirrel again.

"Hey! Cut that out!" Squirrel yelled again.

"I will when you stop those stupid jokes," growled Tommy Gun.

"All right, all right, I'll cut it out," Squirrel whimpered.

"What are we gonna do in a house?" Jana persisted.

"Whatcha think?" Tommy Gun asked. "Take things, o' course."

"But . . . but that's *stealing*," Jana said.

Tommy Gun laughed. "So waddya call what we just did at the Quick Shop? Borrowing?" The rest of the gang laughed. It sounded like a bunch of hyenas.

"I dunno," Jana said, still clearly uneasy. "That just seemed different. Sort of harmless."

"Look, you don't have to take anything," Tommy Gun oozed. "No sweat. Just come along for the ride and watch, if it makes you feel any better."

"Can't I just wait for you guys here?" she asked.

"No! Either you're in, or you're out," Tommy Gun barked. "No in-between."

There was a long, awkward pause as the gang waited for Jana's answer. "Um, okay, I'm in," she murmured. "But I'm not takin' anything. I'm just gonna watch."

"Hey, like I said, no sweat," Tommy Gun said. "Whatever pulls your chain."

The gang climbed aboard their bikes again and headed out. I followed at a distance, my heart sinking. *Why didn't I ever tell Mom.* What they were doing now was *really* breaking the law. Big time. If they got caught, it'd be JD hall for sure.

The gang slowed as they approached a house at the end of a cul-de-sac. The house had the porch light on and one light on downstairs. A sure sign that no one was home.

They all rode their bikes along the side of the house toward the back. I decided to hang out next door, in the shadows. There wasn't much I could do now.

They'd been inside about five minutes when the police cruiser drifted over the top of the hill that led down to the end of the cul-de-sac. It was driving slowly, just its warning lights on. Somebody, a neighbor probably, had tipped them. There was no other reason it would be drifting down the street with its headlights dark and just the hazard lights on.

I started to panic. My sister was inside that house! She was sure to get caught. I could already see the doors of juvenile detention hall starting to slam in Jana's face—

I made my decision in a flash. I'd have to act fast, or I'd be caught right along with them. *That* would sure be an interesting conversation with Mom.

I sprinted across the lawn separating the two houses and found the window they'd all climbed through. I stuck my head inside and yelled, as loud as I dared, "The cops are here! Everybody scram! Now!"

I heard a couple of muffled yells from upstairs, followed by some heavy footsteps on the stairs. I hurried away from the window, my job now done, and ran back to my bike.

I couldn't go back to the street. The cops were sure to see me. So I climbed on my bike and headed out across the backyard of the house next door. I kept to the tree line and pedaled through one backyard after another until I was pretty sure I was well clear of the police cruiser.

I wondered if they'd all gotten out safely. I'd probably given them a head start of about a minute before the police car had arrived. That should have been enough, if they all hurried.

I pedaled back to the park, figuring they'd all go back there to rendezvous. The air was chilly on my cold sweat.

The park was empty when I arrived, but I'd expected that. I circled around it, back toward the woods, and found a choice seat behind some heavy bushes near the fort. I wasn't more than fifteen feet or so from the fort.

The first few members of the gang straggled in a few minutes later. I waited anxiously until Jana arrived. She was one of the last to get there.

"We all here?" Tommy Gun asked.

My eyes had really adjusted to the semidarkness, and I could see Tommy Gun clearly from my vantage point. He was glancing around at his gang members, counting heads.

"Man, that was close," one of the gang said, his chest heaving from the effort. "That cop car was pullin' up just as I was gettin' on my bike..."

"Too close, dude," Tommy Gun nodded. "Good thing one of you had your eyes peeled for the cops and gave us a yell. Who was it?"

There was dead silence. Obviously, I wasn't going to take credit, and the silence stretched off into the darkness.

"Come on!" Tommy Gun said angrily. *"Somebody* warned us! I heard it. Didn't the rest o' y'all hear it too?" Heads bobbed up and down all around.

I stared hard at Jana. Her head wasn't bobbing. Instead, she was looking around her, at the road, at the parking lot, at the woods. She almost looked right at me. I was pretty sure she'd recognized my voice. She knew who'd warned them.

"What's wrong, Jana?" Tommy Gun asked. "Was it you that warned us?"

"No, it wasn't me," Jana said quietly.

Tommy Gun looked at the rest of his gang. "Well, ya morons, who was it?" he yelled. More silence. Clearly, no one was going to step forward.

"Ya bunch o' numbskulls, somebody told us about the cops," Tommy Gun insisted.

"Maybe it was our guardian angel?" somebody volunteered.

"No such thing," growled Tommy Gun. "Now, look, unless somebody . . . "

Tommy Gun never finished his sentence. He stopped, because a car was coming up the road toward them.

"Gotta be those cops!" one of the gang said. "Let's beat it!"

The gang started to scramble. "No, wait!" Tommy Gun ordered. "It ain't the cops. It's just a reg'lar, old car."

The gang stopped, and waited. The car rolled up to the edge of the park and stopped. The headlights flicked off.

For some reason, my heart started to pound. Something awful was about to happen. There were sirens going off in my head. *Nice kids don't cruise at three in the morning on a school night . . .*

Four rough, older kids got out of the car slowly and walked toward the park. I could hear the chains rattling on their boots and their heels click on the pavement as they walked. These guys were serious.

"Yo, party dudes," one of them said as they approached.

"What's happenin', man?" Tommy Gun said bravely.

"Not much," the kid answered. "It's hangin'."

"Cool," Tommy Gun said.

The four new kids came closer. I could see them more clearly now. These were four very ugly, nasty guys. Their clothes looked like they'd been pulled from a trash heap somewhere. They smelled like *they'd* just been pulled from a trash heap.

"You dudes go to Roosevelt?" Squirrel squawked nervously.

"Nah, we split school last year," one of them answered. "Only snot-nose little brats hang out at school."

"Oh," Squirrel said lamely.

I could see Jana starting to ease toward the fort, trying to melt into the background.

"Hey, what we got here?" one of the boys said, spotting Jana. "A little chickadee?"

Jana stopped dead in her tracks. I could feel my flesh starting to crawl. My limbs were almost paralyzed.

"Yo, and she's awful pretty, ain't she?" said the boy, the one who'd spoken first.

"Real nice," said another.

"And sweet," said a third.

Tommy Gun stepped to Jana's side. "Hey, dudes, it's cool. She's with me," he said. I could hear the fear in his voice.

"Not now, she isn't," one of the new boys said, his voice a low growl. "She's ours."

"Hey, come on," Tommy Gun pleaded.

Two knives came out at once. I heard the blades *snap* from where I was sitting.

"Beat it," one of the new boys ordered. "Now!"

Tommy Gun started to edge away from my sister, who was still frozen, like a deer that's been caught in the headlights of an oncoming car. "Dudes, this isn't really—"

"I said *beat* it," one of them growled. "All o' you."

Tommy Gun edged even further away. Jana reached out a tentative hand toward Tommy Gun. He either didn't see it, or refused to take it. Jana was all alone.

"Tommy?" she called out, her voice a pure symphony of terror.

Tommy Gun didn't answer. He was clearly torn. One of the new boys stepped toward Tommy Gun menacingly, his switchblade thrust forward. The rest of the gang started to run to their bikes and flee as fast as they could. Tommy Gun hesitated a moment longer, then turned and ran as well.

Jana moved, finally. She turned to run toward her bike. She was a little too late.

"No, you don't," one of them said, reaching out to grab hold of Jana's long, black hair. "You're stayin' behind."

"To keep us company," a second said.

Jana struggled, as Tommy Gun and his gang vanished into the night. She was now all alone.

Except for me. I was still there. I was scared completely out of my mind, but I wasn't about to leave.

Jana started to cry. "Please, let me go," she begged. "I just wanna go home."

"In a little bit," one of the boys said. "Just relax."

The four boys started to surround Jana. She was crying and whimpering. She was barely even struggling now, so great was her fear.

Oh God, give me strength, I prayed. *Please, God, I need You to hold me up, to help me face this. Stand with me. Be there.*

Almost instantly, my head cleared. My legs and arms lost their paralysis. New hope and strength surged through my body. My fear fled and tumbled away into the night.

I stood up and walked out of the shadows toward my sister. I was strangely unafraid. I had no plan. I just knew I had to do something.

One of the four boys saw me, and turned to face me. "I thought I told you little squirts to beat it," he sneered.

"I'm not one of his gang," I said, my voice unnaturally calm. "I'm her big brother."

The four boys all froze for just an instant, long enough for Jana to break free and bolt toward me, sobbing. She almost collapsed at my side.

"I don't care who you are, kid," one of them said. "You beat it too."

"No," I said defiantly. "I'm not. You'll have to kill me first."

One of the boys held his knife low, out in front. "I think we can manage that," he said, edging toward me.

Jana clung to my arm. I gripped her hand, not sure what would happen next. These guys could cut me in a heartbeat. No question about it.

The two guys with the knives came closer. I stood my ground, holding onto Jana's hand firmly.

"I mean it," I said grimly, my voice steady. "You'll have to kill me. I'm not leaving without my sister."

The two boys didn't answer. They crept closer. They were only two steps away. In just one more moment . . .

"Wait!" said their leader, the one who'd first spoken to Tommy Gun when they'd gotten out of the car. The two with the knives stopped and turned their heads.

"We'll just hurt him a little," one of them said.

"Nah," said the leader. "It ain't worth the grief. We'd have the cops crawlin' all over us. Too many of those little creeps got a good look at us."

The two with the knives turned back to face me. They looked at me, then at Jana, then back at me. "You're lucky, kid," one of them said to me. For good measure, he took a meaningless swipe with his knife. The blade *swished* through the air harmlessly.

"Yeah, and *you're* lucky you got a stupid big brother lookin' out for ya," the other said to my sister.

We stood there like that, staring at each other, for a few seconds more. Jana's death grip on my hand was starting to hurt.

"Come on, let's roll," their leader said at last. "The night's still young."

The four boys turned and walked back to their car slowly, deliberately, their heels clicking and their chains rattling. I watched every step like a hawk, still waiting for them to change their minds.

I don't think I breathed again until they'd started their car and roared away. Jana collapsed in a heap, sobbing. I fell to the ground and put my arms around her. I held her tight. Everything was going to be all right. Jana was safe.

Like "The Capital Crew," Jeffrey Asher Nesbit and his wife and children live near Washington, D.C. Jeff is currently Associate Commissioner for Public Affairs for the U.S. Food and Drug Administration. Before that, he worked as press secretary for Vice-President Dan Quayle and as an investigative reporter in Washington.

Jeff's into sports like Cally, and was the captain of his high school tennis team. When he was a kid, Jeff read all the time, and when he ran out of decent books he promised himself he'd write some himself someday. You'll enjoy his Capital Crew books; he's written others too, like *All the King's Horses* and *Absolutely Perfect Summer* and *The Great Nothing Strikes Back.*

Have you read *Crosscourt Winner?*

. . . Grant hit a high, arcing lob to my backhand side. I reacted quickly, moving to the side to take it with an angled overhead. I cracked it as hard as I could. The ball jumped off my racket. I could see it land just inside the line on the other side for a clear winner.

"Out!" Evan bellowed, holding one forefinger up in the traditional sign indicating he felt the ball had carried long.

I just stood there in shock for a moment. I couldn't believe he was deliberately cheating, on such a crucial point. The ball had been in by several inches. I was sure of it.

I looked up at the court monitor for help. He just shrugged. "He was in a better position to see it," the monitor said. "I can't overrule him, even if I wanted to."

. . . "I never cheat!" Grant yelled. "That ball was out . . . "

"Yeah, sure," I said, turning away. I was so angry my hands were trembling. It would be hard to keep control of my game, now, which is probably what he'd intended.

I took a deep breath before serving. It didn't do any good. My first serve was out by a good foot or so.

. . . The first game of the set was his.

I almost felt like crying as we changed sides. It just wasn't fair. He had cheated, and there was nothing I could do about it.

. . . in the first book of "The Capital Crew," by Jeffrey Asher Nesbit.